THE LIEUTENANT'S MATE

THE BLUE SOLACE: BOOK FOUR

C.W. GRAY

ANCHOR'S REST SYSTEM, CHARYBDIS
STATION

Sebastian Dolarnio kept his eyes closed, smiling softly. He was in his bed, wrapped up in soft sheets. A strong arm lay across his stomach, and he was pressed against a hard body. For the first time in a very long time, he was in bed with a man of his choice. His mate. His body was well-loved, not *used*. Alois's scent surrounded him, and Sebastian scooted back against him.

"Good morning, beautiful," Alois murmured against Sebastian's ear. He nibbled the pointed tip, sending a thread of heat through Sebastian's body. "I missed you so damn much."

"I missed you too," Sebastian replied, rolling in his mate's arms. He cupped Alois's beautiful face. His sweet brown eyes were soft, and the red scales climbing up his neck tickled Sebastian's palms. His Dedril was a handsome man. "But you had a job to do and Wyatt to rescue."

Sebastian knew the physical distance between the

two of them for the past few months had been for the best. It had given them time to talk and get to know one another without the issue of sex getting in the way. Sebastian *knew* Alois now. He knew Alois liked to appear like a silly, irresponsible tomcat, but he wasn't like that at all. He was a bit silly, Sebastian thought with a smile, but he cared deeply about people and was deadly serious about serving Charybdis Station. Alois was a good man – a trustworthy man.

"I hate that I missed Nina's birth. I feel like I've already failed you and her," Alois grumbled and turned his face to kiss Sebastian's palm.

"You would have just passed out if you had been here," Sebastian teased. "We were fine. Leti and the rest of Blue Solace were there in your place."

"It's not the same," Alois said.

"I know," Sebastian said. He had wanted Alois there too. "If we ever have another baby, then we'll try to make sure you're there. Okay?"

"You're placating me," Alois said with a smile. He huffed out a breath. "Fine. We'll just have to have another baby to make sure it happens."

"Hold your horses there, buddy," Sebastian said. "Having babies hurts, and I'm only now able to have sex again. It's going to be a while." He hesitated. "You really didn't mind last night? I'll get better. I promise." Sebastian had thought he was beyond the fear he'd felt from his time on Union Station, but even with Alois, he hadn't been able to handle penetration.

Alois nodded and kissed him. His mouth tingled, and he savored Alois's taste. "You went through a lot, beautiful. It'll take time to heal emotionally and mentally, but I'll be right here beside you."

"What if I can never handle sex?" Sebastian had wanted to be with Alois so badly last night, but he'd frozen, filled with fear at the last second.

"There are a lot of ways to be intimate, beautiful. Remember last night?" Alois nuzzled his nose against Sebastian's. "If you can never handle penetration, it's fine. You're my mate, and I'll treasure you always." Alois kissed him again. After ending the kiss, Alois gave him a mischievous look. "As for babies, if you insist, we'll wait two years. Our house has two extra bedrooms. That means two more babies, right?"

Nina's cries echoed through the baby monitor.

"Why don't we worry about the baby we have?" Sebastian rolled out of bed, happy to see Alois hopping up too. They pulled on pants and went to the newborn's room.

Alois gently picked her up, cradling her in his arms. The light from the window lit up the room, making sparkles dance across her lavendor skin. "She is so beautiful," Alois said in awe. "Look at those eyes. They're just like her papa's."

Sebastian stroked a finger across her cheek. "I never thought something so horrible could create someone so lovely." Her plump face scrunched up with another cry. "I think it's time for a fresh diaper and a bottle."

"I've got this," Alois said confidently. "I've been practicing on Wyatt and Morgan's twins."

He deftly changed the baby's wet diaper while Sebastian got her bottle ready. He handed it to his mate and watched him feed her. A deep satisfaction filled Sebastian at the sight of his man and his daughter.

Alois shot him a look, smiling. "What do you want to do today? Our crew has the next two weeks off since the mission took so long."

"Hmm." Sebastian thought for a minute. "We could go to the trade market. I haven't managed to get there yet since I've been so busy with Leti."

"Have I mentioned how proud I am of you?" Alois leaned over and kissed his cheek. "You are so damn smart. I can't believe you, Leti, and Shae put everything together to figure out the artifact."

"You may have mentioned it a thousand or so times," Sebastian said, blushing. "All I did was translate things." He hadn't done much, but everyone acted like he was a genius. "Leti and Shae did all the hard stuff." They had done the actual research, piecing together the story of the Queen and her elements. He wished he could have helped more, but he wasn't educated like Leti or incredibly smart like Shae.

"You don't give yourself enough credit," Alois said. "One day, you'll see in yourself what we all do. Then we'll all have fun telling you *I told you so*."

"If you say so," Sebastian said, shrugging. Alois and his friends either didn't understand or were being too kind to see the truth. Alois was stuck with him now though, so at least there was that. There would be no abandoning all hope once his mate actually realized who he was mated to.

"I can't wait until that day, beautiful. So, the trade market?" Alois burped Nina and wiped her little face.

"Yes," Sebastian said. "We can drop Nina off at the new daycare center for our sector."

"Who runs it? Do we trust them? Are they able to take care of our girl?" Alois narrowed his eyes and scowled.

"Shae opened it a month ago," Sebastian said, laughing. "He only hires people he completely trusts, and considering he takes care of all of Leti's kids, he knows what he's doing."

"I didn't know he'd opened a daycare," Alois said, surprised.

Shae had been searching for his purpose, his way of aiding Charybdis, for several months now. Sebastian was almost certain the young man had found his place.

"He basically acted as Leti's assistant and nanny for months," Sebastian said. "Then we all got to talking about how it would be awesome to have childcare during attacks. At that point, Leti's house was the place to drop off your kids before heading out. As large as it is, it's just one house."

"Shae's found his purpose," Alois said with a smile. "That's awesome."

"It is," Sebastian agreed. "He isn't a fighter, medic, or diplomat, but he can sure as hell handle baby chaos."

"Leti's out an assistant then?"

"Shae still has time to help out," Sebastian said. "He has a lot of help at the daycare. I even go in when I can." He hadn't had much time until recently, he thought, feeling guilty. He'd spent every spare minute translating Ancient Crellic for Leti.

"Let's go, beautiful," Alois said, searching through

the dresser for clothes for Nina. "I want to see what has changed in our sector. I was only here for about a week before we left, but I noticed it's grown like crazy."

"It has," Sebastian agreed.

Leti's father-in-law had built the neighborhood solely for Leti. He had wanted his new son to be close to his friends. The new sector they lived in had been built when Charybdis Station made the shift from mercenary group to planetary government. Since then, the Blue sector had really taken off, shifting from simple mercenary barracks and military-like housing to true homes. Backyards and community gardens were springing up everywhere.

Alois quickly dressed their girl in a pink dress with white and purple flowers on it. They showered and dressed, then left the house.

"I'm hungry," Alois said, and Sebastian heard his stomach rumble. His own gave an answering growl, and both men laughed. Nina sniffled from the baby sling strapped to Alois's chest.

"Well, since we have empty stomachs, I have another surprise for you," Sebastian said. "Come on."

He held Alois's hand as they walked two blocks over. Juniper's Diner matched the surrounding buildings, smooth and grey, but flowers filled the baskets in the window, while planters full of more flowers lined the walk. A speckled chicken sat in one of the planters and watched people as they walked by, and a large rooster strutted up and down the patch of grass in front of the window, occasionally crowing to remind everyone it was morning.

"Fuck me," Alois said. "Juniper opened a restaurant?"

"Yeah. He ran our sector's gardens for a while, but he missed cooking too much. He figured he could make a living cooking for Leti and the rest of us." Sebastian nodded to the chicken. "Good morning, Miss Speckles."

"He'll make a ton of money off us," Alois said, rushing inside. "I can't wait for good food. You have no idea how horrible it is to not have a cook onboard."

"Sebastian and Alois," Juniper said, hands full of plates. "Look who finally got out of bed." The man smirked and delivered breakfast to a table full of Blue Solace crewmembers.

"Hey, guys," Dru said, nodding. Her newt, Monty, was curled up on her shoulder. "You two missed out on an awesome dinner last night at Leti's." She smiled slyly. "I guess you had more important things to do."

"Sweet mama, be nice to the new couple," said her husband, Lerais. He took her hand. "You remember those first few months, don't you?"

Her eyes grew warm. "Hell yeah," she said, licking her lips. "Those were some fine times."

"You two are disturbing the other diners," Juniper said. Cordelia, Hazel, and Linc did look disturbed… and slightly nauseated.

"Sebastian," Leti called out from his table. "Bring Alois over here and eat with us." His friend waved energetically.

Though Leti was just as integral to Blue Solace as any of the rest of the crew, he stood out. Alois and the others in the restaurant were dressed in their severe, black and blue uniforms, while Leti wore a soft button-up sweater, covered in playful raccoons over a plain white shirt stretched tight over his huge belly. He was hard to overlook, especially with the travel-sized Fire Veil Dragon on his shoulder.

Sebastian pulled Alois behind him and sat in an empty chair at Leti's table. Wyatt and Morgan sat on one side with Wyatt's father, and Leti and Grandpa Moses—along with a herd of kids—took up the other side. Sebastian had grown very fond of Grandpa Moses in the month he had been there. The old man was a bit crazy, but he loved his family to distraction.

"How's that baby?" Moses asked, reaching out and unstrapping Nina from Alois's chest, startling Sebastian's man. He cuddled the little girl close. "My sweet girl."

"Don't worry," Morgan said to Alois. "He says that about all the baby girls."

Sebastian laughed when he noticed the elderly man had Wyatt's twins on one side of him and Pepper on the other. He was surrounded by baby girls.

"I love my grandsons too," Moses protested, patting Sami on the head. The little boy leaned into Leti's side but grinned up at his grandpa.

"Sebastian, if you ever aren't happy with Alois," Morgan said. "I have this friend who's single. He's a really nice guy. Likes kids." He smiled sweetly even as he batted his eyes at Alois. The small baby Frost Veil Dragon on his head batted his own eyes too and cooed.

"You can keep your single friends to yourself," Alois

said, wrapping an arm around Sebastian's shoulders and grinning. "Sebastian is mated now."

Sebastian laughed when Stardust hissed, and a puff of cold air filled the air around Morgan's head. "I'll take Stardust though."

"Not my baby," Morgan said, patting his little dragon. "Princess is already convinced he's Stardust's daddy."

Moses ignored Morgan and eyed Alois. "Sebastian is a good boy. You'll be living with him and taking care of his little girl, right?"

"Nina is *our* little girl," Alois answered. "I'm moving my stuff to our house tonight, and I don't plan on going anywhere."

"Good," Moses said, smiling softly. "What are you up to today, Sebastian? Are you finally taking a break?"

"Yes, sir," he said smartly. "Alois and I are going to drop Nina off at Shae's, then go to the trade market."

"Oh, that sounds fun," Leti said. He rubbed his huge belly. "I'm too tired to go or I'd tag along with you. I hear they have these beautiful birds for sale at one of the stalls."

"No more pets for you," Moses said firmly. "The desert knows you have the heart to love any and every being in the galaxy, but your home is only so big."

"Maybe I was thinking about Sebastian," Leti said defensively. "He doesn't have any pets at all."

Sebastian struggled to hide his smile. He had never had a pet before and wasn't sure how he felt about it. He could already see Leti piling him up with animals since his own house was already overflowing.

"Sure, you were," Moses said, then turned back to Sebastian. "I'll watch Ms. Nina for you. I didn't get to sing to her yesterday since her papa and daddy were getting reacquainted."

Sebastian blushed again. Damn them.

"What about you, Wyatt?" Sebastian was so happy to finally see his friend in person.

"We're going to spend some time with the twins today while Estella is in school," Wyatt said, eyes sparkling with happiness. "I have a feeling you two could stand some alone time."

Sebastian made a face at him and their friends laughed.

After a delicious breakfast, Sebastian kissed Nina goodbye and left her with Moses. Then, he headed to the shuttle tram with his mate. They passed Shae's Daycare, and Sebastian smiled when they peeked through the big front window. Shae sat surrounded by kids. He was reading a book and each child looked enthralled.

Hmm, maybe they are, Sebastian thought. Sirens could do some crazy shit.

"Alright," Alois said. "Nina can stay here when she's not with Moses."

Sebastian arched an eyebrow. "I'm sure Shae would appreciate your approval. Come on. We don't want to miss the tram."

They made it to the tram and got on, heading toward the market. "This place really has grown," Alois said. "I knew we were taking in a lot of refugees, but damn."

"According to Hack, as soon as the rest of the system knew Charybdis Station was leaving behind its mercenary status, the Lord Admiral started receiving a lot of requests to move here. Charybdis has the best medical research facilities in the galaxy, not to mention their engineering development," Sebastian said. "He had to start a whole new department of the new government to deal with immigration. I heard they're even talking about starting a university here. Crazy, huh?" They arrived at the trade market, and Sebastian gasped. "How have I never been here before?"

"You've been a little busy," Alois said with a grin. "Come on, beautiful. People travel across systems to see this place."

The market stalls stretched for miles and sold products from all over the galaxy. Sebastian saw Fallon silk, Betonize weapons, and Silet paintings and pottery. He couldn't resist a small, ceramic vase. It was brightly colored, and he knew it would look gorgeous in the living room.

"I'll get that," Alois said, taking the vase.

"I have money," Sebastian said defensively. He hated it, but Charybdis Station paid him a salary to translate Ancient Crellic for Leti. He had a few books left to go, as well as several data cubes.

"I know," Alois said, shrugging. "I just want to buy something for the house. It's for the living room, right? It'll look so good there."

Sebastian smiled. It was easy to forget that it was Alois's house now too. "Sorry. Money is an issue for me. I'm used to not having anything, and now I have a good amount saved up since the Lord Admiral won't let me pay rent."

"He won't let any of us pay rent," Alois said. "He told us our new homes were a gift. The mercenary business pays well, and he wanted to do something for Leti."

"Well, he's not a mercenary general anymore," Sebastian said, frustration bleeding through. "He shouldn't go blowing his money on us."

"Beautiful, you can't tell that man anything," Alois said. "He's been the unofficial dad to the Blue Solace crew for so long, he wouldn't know what to do if he had to stop."

Sebastian groaned. "He's an overprotective menace. Do you know that Renee and he insisted on staying with me the first two weeks after Nina was born? He said he was worried I'd get overwhelmed as a single parent." *Not that I didn't fully appreciated it*, Sebastian thought. "As soon as they left, Ma and Pops came to stay for another two weeks. Then, each of *your* friends took turns spending the night. I haven't been alone since Nina was born, and I now know that Selene is obsessed with weapons. Did you notice the daggers displayed in the guest bathroom?"

"It doesn't surprise me," Alois said, snorting, then continued talking. Sebastian knew his mate was speaking, but he didn't hear him anymore.

At one of the stalls were the most beautiful creatures Sebastian had ever seen. They were birds but not like any he recognized. They were each a completely different combination of colors and had long, delicate tail feathers that touched the ground from where they perched. They had elaborate plumage and thick bodies, and Sebastian knew they had to weigh more than Biscuit, Cordelia's little dog.

"Sebastian?" Alois waved a hand in front of his eyes, then followed his gaze to the birds. "Uh oh. Leti's influence is too strong. Resist."

One of the birds stood out from the others. He was blue, green, and purple, and the tip of his tail feathers were black and gold. His luminous golden eyes stared straight at Sebastian. "I need him," Sebastian said. "He's mine."

Alois sighed and pulled him over to the stall. "What kind of birds are these and how much does that one cost?"

2

*A*lois fed Nina as he watched Sebastian get his bird settled into its new, elaborate home. The vendor had explained the bird was a Radollia from Grellweir and was a companion pet. The bird looked like a pampered princess.

Alois watched as Sebastian made sure the cage door was pinned open. They had already set up several perches throughout the house since the vendor told them all his birds were house trained. Alois doubted that was possible. He remembered Dannol's rooster and Juniper's hen and the bird poop everywhere.

"Isn't he beautiful, Alois?" Sebastian's voice was dreamy, and he clearly loved the damn thing.

Alois sighed. He'd deal with it. "Yeah. What are you going to call it?"

"It?" Sebastian gave him a dark look and propped his hand on his hip. "Mustachio isn't an *it*. He is a *he*."

"Mustachio?" Alois tilted his head, considering the

bird. That was a weird name. He shrugged and went back to feeding his little girl. Mustachio ignored him in return and continued cleaning his feathers.

Sebastian put fresh berries and vegetables next to the raw bits of chicken in the ornate food dish. *Damn bird ate better than I did on my last mission*, Alois thought grumpily.

"Now, we just leave him to get used to his new home," Sebastian said. "I should make sure the windows are closed. Leti, Draif, and I took down the fence separating our yards, and sometimes Wobble pokes his head in the kitchen. I'll be right back, my sweet boy."

He ran off, and Alois considered the bird. "Nina, I have a feeling this is your new brother."

"Alois, come here," Sebastian called. "You need to see this."

"What is it?" Alois walked to the kitchen and stood next to Sebastian. He had a perfect view into Leti's back yard. Leti's guard, Silas, lay in the hammock, body entwined with Rune's. They simply lay sleeping together, but it was the sweetest thing he'd ever seen. "That is adorable. Let me take pictures and send it to everyone."

Sebastian shook his head. "You all are ridiculous. Always trying to embarrass each other."

"That," Alois said, pointing at the sleeping couple, "isn't embarrassing. It's beautiful and needs to be seen by the galaxy. Just like my little Nina's pictures." He sent everyone the picture, then turned back to

Sebastian. He leaned forward and kissed his mate. Gods, he had missed him. Sebastian kissed him back, and things started getting heated until they heard the doorbell.

Sebastian groaned. "Damn people and their need to be our friends."

"How dare they?" Alois tilted his head back, nose in the air, and strode to the front door, Nina cuddled to his chest. He narrowed his eyes at Cordelia. "May I help you?"

"Oh, I'm sorry," she said. "Did I interrupt your spying session?"

"Yes. Yes, you did."

"Deal with it," she said, bouncing foot to foot. "I have a problem."

"Come on in, Cordy girl," Alois said, opening the door. His friend pushed in and stopped, staring at Mustachio. Biscuit paused beside her and tilted his head, whining.

"What is *that?*"

"Cordelia," Sebastian said, gasping. "Mustachio is my sweet boy and deserves respect."

She sent Alois a sympathetic look. "He really spent a lot of time with Leti. I'm sorry."

"It's one bird," Alois said, shrugging. "Mustachio makes him happy."

A loud banging came from the kitchen, and Sebastian jumped. "Damn it. I forgot Wobble always gets an afternoon snack. He's probably not happy about the window being closed."

Alois stifled his laughter as his mate ran to the

kitchen. "Come on, Cordy. Let's sit and you can tell Alois all your problems."

The petite blonde rolled her eyes and threw herself into a chair. Biscuit hopped up into her lap. "Quinn asked me out."

"Oh, no," Alois said, voice full of dread. "A beautiful woman asked you out. How horrible."

"Shut up," Cordelia said, snarling. "The problem is, apparently everyone but me knew Quinn has a thing for me."

"I still don't see the problem," Alois said.

"I really like her," Cordelia said. "She's a good soldier and a really good friend. I don't want to lose that friendship."

"Oh," Alois said, drawing the word out. "Did you tell her that?"

"Yes," Cordelia said with a sigh. "I feel like shit. Her eyes just dimmed, man. Now the whole crew will hate me."

"Hey now," Alois said, sitting on the ottoman in front of her chair. "You get to make your own decisions. I know Quinn wouldn't want you to go out with her just because the crew expected it."

"That's part of the problem. I really like her, and I know we'd be good together."

"Cordy," Alois said, smacking her arm. "Why not take a risk?"

"I'd probably mess it up," she said, grumbling. "Right now, I can't imagine a morning without a chat with Quinn. I won't chance it."

"Okay," Alois said, shrugging. He'd give her a few months, then push and prod her again.

"It gets worse," she said, slumping.

"Uh oh. Lay it on me."

"We're training together this morning."

"That's good," Alois said.

"What?" Cordelia gave him a look of disbelief. "Did you not just hear me? It's going to be so damn awkward."

"It will," Alois agreed, nodding. "For the first few days. Then, you two will talk and work it out."

"How do you know that?"

"Because you are both adults with at least a little bit of intelligence and maturity," he said. "Cordelia, you hurt her feelings, but you care about her. That will help you both to move on. I know she has a huge crush on you, we tease her about it mercilessly, but she'll find someone who adores her. So, will you."

"Okay," Cordelia said, panic easing from her eyes. "I can do this."

"I'll tell the crew to back off," Alois said. "We're a nosy bunch, but we don't want to hurt anyone."

"Thanks, Alois," Cordelia said. "Alright. I have to pick up dog food for Biscuit and do a shift at Shae's." She stood. "I really missed you. I never realized how much time we spent together until you were gone."

Alois pulled her into a hug. "I missed you too, Cordy."

A deep trill sounded from their left, and they turned to look at Mustachio as the bird sang. His voice was deeper than most birds Alois had heard, but clear and beautiful. His song was sweet and happy, almost encouraging.

"Okay. I love Mustachio now too," Cordelia said.

"Is that him? Oh, he's so beautiful," Sebastian said, coming into the room. Alois glared at the bird. Sebastian should be saying that *Alois* was beautiful.

Cordelia chuckled. "You're jealous of a bird." She pulled her comm out. "Wait until everyone hears this." Alois gave her a flat look, but she just laughed and ran out the door, Biscuit woofing at her heels.

"Aww," Sebastian said, swaying to Mustachio's song. He gave Alois a coy look. "Are you jealous, handsome?"

"Yes," Alois pouted. "I'm beautiful."

"You are," Sebastian agreed, moving closer to him.

"I can sing too," Alois said defensively. He didn't sing *well*, but he could sing.

"I would love to hear you one day," Sebastian said, wrapping his arms around Alois's waist. His head just reached the middle of Alois's chest, and his ear settled against Alois's heart.

"The stupid bird does sound good," Alois grumbled. He carefully balanced Nina as he wrapped an arm around his mate, resting his chin on top of Sebastian's head. "I guess it's not too bad."

———

LATER THAT NIGHT, Alois finished tucking Nina in and watched her sleep for a moment. He had never imagined his life would be so full, so happy. He had always wanted a life-mate, the one person in all the galaxy that was meant to be his. His father and mother had not been mates. They would use it as an excuse to slip up and sleep with anyone that caught their eye. Alois hated the pain the betrayals caused, but they just did it over and over again, until any love they had once felt for each other was gone.

Alois shook himself. He hated thinking of them and their self-induced misery. At least he had been an only child. He swallowed. He had a mate, so he would never have to worry about that. He thought of Sebastian and smiled. Even if they hadn't been mates, he would have trusted his man. After talking to him for months, Alois knew Sebastian was a loyal and honest person. Alois could trust his heart to him, mate or not.

Mustachio slept on the perch in the hallway outside Nina's room, so Alois closed the door quietly, visions of the bird feasting on his baby girl filling his mind. He eyed the bird as he walked across the hall to their bedroom.

"Stop glaring at Mustachio," Sebastian said from the bed. He lay spread out, robe falling open. "The vendor said all his birds were trained to react well around children and other pets."

"I don't want him to eat Nina," Alois said, eyes roaming over his mate. He slowly undressed, appreciating the passion growing in Sebastian's eyes. He slid his pants to the floor and crawled across the bed.

Sebastian put a hand to the back of Alois's neck and pulled him down for a kiss. "Have I told you lately how much I adore you?" Sebastian asked, breaking the kiss.

"You were so sweet to Cordelia. I love how your friends come straight to you for advice, even if they don't realize they're doing it half the time."

"They're a crazy bunch," Alois said. "I love them anyway, just, uh, don't tell them that."

"Me too," Sebastian said. He stroked his face. "I'm worried, Alois. Everything that's happening is so crazy, so big. I don't want this to change."

"What do you mean?"

"I have this feeling, in my gut, that the galaxy is about to be turned on its head," Sebastian said. "I don't know why I feel it. We have a strong ally, and we've killed two of the Queen's most powerful weapons. We're holding our own, but I just feel like there's more somehow. I just want to be right here though. You in my bed and Nina happy and safe."

"Nothing is ever certain, beautiful," Alois said, struggling to shake off the feeling that Sebastian was right. "One thing we can be certain of is no matter what comes, we'll face it together." Alois sank down beside him and focused on loving his mate.

He licked a path down Sebastian's body, pushing his mate's robe open as he went. When he reached his dick, Alois stroked him, then kissed the tip. "May I, beautiful?"

"You may," Sebastian said, smiling and panting.

Alois hummed in appreciation and swallowed Sebastian's dick.

"Oh, fuck."

Alois bobbed his head, working Sebastian's cock and watching his mate's face closely. There was no fear, only lust and love. Sebastian held his head as he came, groaning deeply.

"Dear god, that was so good," he said, stroking Alois's hair. Warmth filled his eyes, and he gave Alois a small, secret smile. "My turn."

3

Sebastian watched as Alois fed Nina the next morning. "Am I ever going to hold my daughter again?"

"No," Alois said. "She's my girl." He burped her and laid her back in her bed.

"You'll have to go back to work one day," Sebastian said, thoughtfully. "I'll get her then." His comm chimed, and he looked at it. *Blah!* Then again. He rejected the call, then looked back at Alois.

"Nope. I'm taking her everywhere with me. If Hack can have a baby on his lap during a space battle, so can I."

Sebastian laughed. "We'll see what Dru says about that." Mustachio flew into the nursery, sitting on the edge of Nina's bed. He sang a low, soft song.

"He wants to eat Nina," Alois said, frowning at the bird.

"No, he doesn't," Sebastian said, exasperated. "Mustachio is singing her a lullaby."

"We'll see," Alois said, eyes narrowed. "I'm not leaving the room."

"I'm going to Leti's house to work for a bit." He pointed between Mustachio and Alois. "You two behave."

"Yes, dear," Alois said, eyes trained on the bird. Sebastian rolled his eyes and left his idiot mate to it.

Sebastian left the house and followed the little pebble-covered trail from his front door to Leti's. Juniper had planted pink deutzia bushes along the trail, and they were in full bloom. Leti waited at the door. His belly looked even bigger than yesterday, and the poor man looked miserable. Sami peeked around his leg, flashing baby fangs when he smiled at Sebastian and waved. Another year and the little boy would be heading to school.

"This baby needs to come out," Leti said, close to tears. "Right now."

"Are you in labor?" Sebastian pulled up his comm, ready to call for Nettle and Lilah. "You still have another week."

"No," Leti wailed. "The baby won't come out, and I want him out right fucking now."

Sebastian breathed a sigh of relief. "One more week, Leti. He'll come soon enough. Have you picked a name yet?" He picked up Sami and turned Leti toward the house, pushing him a bit to get him moving.

"No," Leti said, grumpiness in his voice. "Will and I can't agree on a name. I don't want to call him Willard Jr."

Sebastian laughed as he set Sami back down. The

little boy ran to his Betonize hunting cat, Pax, and squatted in front of him, petting his ears and nose.

"There's nothing wrong with Willard Jr.," Moses said. The man stood in the kitchen doorway, Pepper balanced on his hip. "Come on, sweet Sami. Do you want to go to the park?"

"Park!" Sami yelled and shimmied, dancing in place. "Pax come with."

"Okay," Moses agreed. "Go find his leash." The little boy ran to the living room, and Moses kissed the top of Leti's head. "You relax some today, alright? That boy will come soon enough."

Leti groaned. "Why do you have to be so sweet and logical? Why?" Sami came back into the room with a leash. "Pick him up, Sebastian. Please? I want to kiss him goodbye." Sebastian tried not to laugh as he grabbed Sami again. Leti leaned over and gave Pepper and Moses both a big smooch, then tickled Sami's belly and kissed him too. "You all have fun. I'm going to nap while Uncle Sebastian does all the work."

Moses, Pax, and the kids left, and Sebastian followed Leti to his office. The little space was just like Leti – chaotic, warm, and comforting. Druffle ran through the tunnels lining the wall. They were especially active today, he noted. Sebastian walked past a dozing Princess Buttercup and settled at his desk in one corner. It was piled high with books and data cubes and had two small vid-screens. Sebastian settled in his seat.

"If you don't mind, I really am going to take a nap," Leti said. He yawned and rubbed his eyes.

"You need the rest," Sebastian said, smiling. "Princess needs a snuggle buddy too." The ten-foot dragon opened his eyes and a puff of smoke curled from his nostrils. Sebastian shivered. Princess was a bit intimidating.

"I'll get you a cup of tea and some snacks first," Leti said, already half-way out the door.

"You don't have to… and he's gone," Sebastian said. He shrugged and looked through the stack of books left to translate. "Hmm. Here's another book of mythology, Princess." His head spun back to Princess. He noticed the tiny white and blue Frost Veil Dragon curled up on Princess's back. "Aww, Stardust. Are you visiting with Daddy Princess today? Fuck. That's a weird title."

He turned his attention back to the book and flipped through the first few pages. "Wait. This is really old." It looked like it was from before the last two of the Queen's cycles. "Let's start here." He started with the title page, then moved to the table of contents and prologue.

"Here you go," Leti said, startling him. His friend set a platter of veggies and little sandwiches on the corner of his desk. A steaming cup of black tea with honey perched in the middle. "Princess, Stardust, and I will be upstairs in bed. Come get me if you need me." He patted Sebastian's shoulder and left him to his book.

Hours later, Sebastian's platter of snacks was gone, and he was on his third cup of tea. The book wasn't a book of myths. It was a history book focused on the details of the Queen's original life. It cited sources they would never have access to, but it didn't sugarcoat the Queen or her elements' lives. At the time of this author, his leaders were debating trying to resurrect her. The author didn't seem to be in favor of it.

He sighed. Death told them all about her beginnings, so this wasn't really new information. He looked at the faded, inked picture of the Queen standing in a beautiful flower garden. She held the hand of a man, and they looked at one another with such love. He recognized Earth's markings.

Sebastian brought up a far more recent picture of the Queen on the vid-screen. She stood on a battlefield looking around her with joy. Earth stood behind her, directly to her left, head bowed in subservience. Life stood to her right, head raised and expression smug. Sebastian wiped his eyes. The Queen really had been someone completely different when she first lived. Poor Earth shared her love in his first life, then was forced to watch her take Life as a lover each time they were brought back. He wouldn't be able to handle that if it was Alois and him.

He flipped back a few pages, reading the account of Water's rebellion. According to the primary sources from that time, the element had grown bored. He ran away, as far as he could, and started *drinking* people. The Queen and the others found him and stopped him, but thousands had died. There was a picture of him bowing in front of the Queen, her face full of disgust and anger. The account went on to say that Water's rebellion inspired one from Air. The element created horrendous storms that killed thousands. Again, the

Queen chased him down and stopped him, angered by his disregard for living beings.

"Life was still the worst," he whispered aloud. That particular element hadn't needed to run away to do damage. He had wreaked havoc in the Queen's tribe. One account of his cruelty stood out from the others. One of the Queen's favorite warriors found his life-mate, a young peasant woman. Life took advantage of her self-doubt as a new member of a wealthy tribe and took control of her. He made her have sex with every person that was willing, essentially raping her.

Her unexplained actions broke her mate's heart. The man hadn't known she wasn't in control of her body until the Queen figured it out and explained it to him. Life was punished, but the damage was done. The warrior took his mate and left the Queen's tribe, heart full of hatred. Another war began. The Queen won, but barely.

Sebastian nibbled his lip. The Queen fought for peace, either through negotiation or battle. He looked again at the picture on the screen. What kind of screwed-up spell could taint the soul so much it turned a decent person into a monster?

"Are you still working?" Leti moved slowly and sat in the window seat. "Grandpa Moses and the kids got back hours ago. Will is going to be home in just a few minutes, and Ma came over to cook dinner."

Sebastian sat back, stretching his arms above his head. "Is it bad that I feel sorry for the Queen?"

Leti looked thoughtful. "What did you find?"

"Confirmation on what Death told us," Sebastian

said. "It's one thing to hear a quick summary, but another to read tons of detailed accounts about her life." He gave Leti an agonized look. "I think she and Earth were somehow life-mates, just like you and Hack. Like Alois and me. Can you imagine the pain Earth must be in?"

"He still serves her," Leti said softly. "I see what you mean though. If Will was forcibly changed into a monster, it would kill me. It's not a simple situation."

Sebastian sighed. "Maybe we should just focus on how the Queen is now. It will make it easier to kill her, and I guess that *should* be our focus."

Leti watched him, considering. "Keep digging, Sebastian. Every bit of knowledge we find will lead us to the answer."

"Will do," he said. "I may just take a break from this book and start another one too. It'll clear my mind."

"I'll call your man and tell him to get over here. I did mention that Ma's cooking, right?"

Sebastian laughed. "You did and my belly says, *thank the gods*."

Leti left, and Sebastian grabbed a book from his pack, looking at the familiar cover guiltily. He traced his finger over the odd symbol on the front. It was a compilation of the symbols of all the elements. He should turn it and the translation over to Leti, but he didn't want to part with it. Not yet.

He heard a whoosh of wind, and Mustachio landed on the windowsill. He preened, trilling hello. "Mustachio," Sebastian said. "Why are you outside?

You're an indoor birdie. Did Alois dump you outside? Hmm, did you eat Alois?"

"Oh, what is that?" Leti eyed Mustachio in appreciation.

"He's mine," Sebastian said. "He's a companion bird. Isn't he beautiful?"

"He's gorgeous. I've never had a bird before, you know," Leti said.

"No." Hack lounged in the doorway and watched Leti and Sebastian stroke Mustachio's feathers. "No more pets."

"This one is mine," Sebastian said.

"I make no promises." Leti waddled to his mate and kissed him. "I've never had a bird, Will."

Hack groaned. "Ma said dinner was ready." He looked at Sebastian. "Alois is here, and he said your damn bird flew out the window while he was feeding Wobble some apples. I guess we know where he went."

They filed toward the kitchen, and Mustachio flew above them, landing on the open windowsill in Leti's kitchen. Sebastian noted Alois's breath of relief and tried not to laugh. "Did you try to get my bird to run away?"

"No, beautiful," Alois said, looking stricken. "I know you love that damn bird."

"I'm just kidding, Alois," Sebastian said with a laugh. He kissed him softly, then stroked Nina's head. Alois held their daughter as usual. "I think he'll follow us right home."

"He's so lovely," Ma said and fed Mustachio a bit of broccoli. "I haven't seen a Radollia since the last time we visited Grellweir. They're good companions, Sebastian, and utterly loyal. I don't think you'll have to worry about him running away."

"He eats too well to leave you, beautiful," Alois said, eating a bite of his own meal.

Ma's belly laugh filled the room. "That's what my honey bear says about himself." She sat beside her husband, shooting him an amused look.

Pops looked sheepish but smiled wide. "It's true. You cook too well for me to want to leave." The large man took her smaller, yellow hand in his. "Who am I kidding? You could cook as bad as Leti and I'd still never leave you."

"Pops," Leti said, looking devastated. "I'm the lowest standard of comparison now?"

"When cooking's the topic, sweet pea," Pops said, taking a bite of his potatoes. "You have many talents, but cooking isn't one of them."

"I can't believe you said that," Leti said. He looked around the table. "It's not true, right?" Sebastian stared at his plate and shoveled food in his mouth. Maybe if he didn't make eye contact. "Sebastian?"

He peeked at Leti. "I love you, Leti. You, Shae, and Wyatt are my best friends, and I believe in you. One day, you'll be a great cook."

Leti sat up straight. "One day." He looked around. "You'll all see."

4

Alois took pictures through the window. Silas and Rune were snuggling on the hammock again. This time, Abbot was with them. Mo's big jackrabbit sat atop their stomachs, settled in to rest. Sebastian sat at the kitchen table, books and his tablet spread out in front of him. A steaming cup of tea sat on a saucer nearby, and he watched Alois.

"Are you spying on Silas and Rune again?"

"Maybe," Alois said. "They're just so damn cute."

Sebastian just laughed and went back to the book he was translating. He'd been fascinated by it all week. Alois smiled at his mate, then sent the pictures to his friends. "Nina and I will be back by lunch," he said. "Unless we decide to go shopping."

"I can't believe you're taking her to a mandatory meeting," Sebastian said, rolling his eyes. "You could part with her for one morning."

"No," Alois said. "She's my girl."

"So, I've heard," Sebastian said. He leaned up and

pulled Alois down to give him a kiss. "You two have fun after the meeting and feel free to call me if she gets to be too much."

Alois kissed him again. He would never get enough of Sebastian's taste. "Enjoy your books," he said finally, licking the taste of his mate from his lips.

Sebastian looked a bit dazed. Mustachio flew into the room and landed gracefully on the perch in the corner. He started to hum. Alois shook his hand and grabbed Nina's bag while Sebastian cooed to their little girl. She was strapped securely in her stroller, dressed in a white pantsuit covered with colorful baby bunnies – a gift from Leti. Sebastian tucked a soft, purple knitted blanket around her, then walked them to the door.

Alois kissed his mate one more time, then headed to the tram. Dru told everyone last night that the Lord Admiral wanted to meet briefly this morning for an update on the station. It didn't take long to get to the admiral's district, and Nina and he strolled into the conference room, right on time. Dru rolled her eyes when she saw Nina but couldn't resist giving her a kiss and unstrapping her from the stroller. Alois sat between her and Cordelia, setting Nina's bag at his feet.

Lord Admiral Fasi Juren paced at the front of the room, face stern but a little worried. His wife, Renee, the security chief for the station, stood calmly at the front of the large table.

Hack plopped into the seat next to Dru and leaned around her to smile at Alois. "Nice picture of Silas and

Rune. They barely leave Silas's room. Rune says it's because Silas needs help healing."

Alois laughed. "I'm sure that's it."

"Alright," Fasi said, coming to stand next to Renee. "I think everyone's here. Renee and I are meeting with each sector today to personally update you on what is happening in regard to the Concords and the elements. I want to hear your ideas, so please speak up."

"The first concern we wanted to discuss is the two elements that are in our possession," Renee said. Fortunately, Alois's friends had been able to kill both Water and Life, and their essences retreated to the artifacts that housed them. Now they sat in a lab, protected by Charybdis Station's best.

"What are your thoughts?" Fasi looked around at the crowd of the Blue Fleet's officers and Hack's personal crew of the Blue Solace. "Please keep in mind that our enforcers have already stopped two attempted thefts of the artifacts."

Alois thought about Sebastian's stories last night. Water, Air, and Life were bad from the start. Sebastian thought it had something to do with their original creation, but that was all supposition. There was no doubt they were dangerous and lacked any compassion.

"Can we use them?" Draif leaned forward, face thoughtful. Leti's best friend was now a captain of his own ship and crew. His insight and skills had impressed the whole station. "They're both very powerful and could be useful."

Fasi looked conflicted. "That was one suggestion

the Council made. Both elements have interesting powers that no species has ever seen before. Damn it, but the idea makes me sick."

"Sebastian has been translating a new book that tells the historic accounts of their original lives," Alois said, hesitant to speak but knowing they needed the information. "Death told us Air, Water, and Life were cruel from the start, and he was right. If their Queen had trouble controlling them, how would we manage it? I suggest we let Wyatt and his father figure out a way to permanently destroy them."

"They've already caused so much damage, and they've only been active for a little over a year," Draif said thoughtfully. "That might be the best choice."

"Could they be turned to our side like Death?" asked Finn, Hack's lieutenant.

"I don't think so," Hack said. "Death has Wyatt as a connection to us. His situation is also a little unique. He isn't just Death. He's also Dr. Morrick."

"If we can't control them, and they won't willingly ally with us, why wouldn't we kill them?" Finn shrugged. "If they were any other species and had committed the acts they have, we would have executed them."

"Technically, we did," Dru said, stroking Monty's head. The newt was perched on her shoulder. "We just need to take that extra step and make it permanent."

"Bringing them back would mean doing the rituals too," said Lucas, Draif's lieutenant. "That means killing two people and ripping their souls from their bodies." He shuddered.

"Excellent point," Fasi said. He huffed a breath out. "I'll talk to everyone today, but I am certainly leaning toward a permanent ending for those two. The Council is split on the issue, but I'm the one making the decision."

"I'll get Sebastian to send you the accounts he already translated," Alois said. "Read a few of them to the Council, and that will convince them."

Fasi nodded. "Alright. The next topic we wanted to discuss is the Half-Moon Assassins Guild. Guild Leader Beol has agreed to move to Charybdis Station and integrate his guild with our station. We have a plan but are still arguing the details. Again, the Council is divided."

"Beol is good people," Dru said, stroking her new vibro-blade – a reluctant gift from Beol.

"He's an assassin though," Beck said. "What if someone pays him to kill someone on Charybdis Station?"

"One of the provisions that we've already agreed on prevents him from taking a contract for any Charybdis Station citizen," Renee said.

"It's seems like a potential political nightmare," Draif said. "What happens when their enemies decide they're now Charybdis Station's enemies?" He thought for a moment. "The income from their guild would be good for the station though."

Fasi gave them a funny smile. Alois frowned. His leader had a secret. "I'm working on convincing Beol to agree to a few things that will allow them to settle in well. We'll come back to that, though if you have any ideas, send them my way. The Half-Moon Assassins *are* coming to the station. That's not up for argument. They've already agreed to work with us against the Queen and her elements in exchange for a new home. Wolfe's team is in the Crellic System, keeping an eye on the Queen on Genarg. They've also agreed to provide us with their tech."

"Oh," Beck said, eyes widening. "They have some damn fine shields. You should definitely let them live here, Lord Admiral."

Fasi laughed. "We know where your heart is, Beck."

Renee cleared her throat, sending Beck a fond look. "That brings us to our next topic. Fasi has been in constant discussion with the leaders of each planet in our system. *All* of the planets in Anchor's Rest are joining together to defend the system." Alois's jaw dropped, and everyone in the room seemed just as shocked as he was. While the planets got along fairly well, this was a huge step.

"Together, we will form a unit called the Anchor's Rest Defense Force," Fasi said. "Each planet, including us, will send soldiers to man it. The primary goal of this force will be to keep the planets in Anchor's Rest safe."

"What happens when two planets decide to go to war," Draif asked. "It would need to be a completely neutral body to be effective."

"Yes," Fasi agreed. "It would. If war was to happen, the leader of this force would have to maintain the peace among his soldiers. It wouldn't be an easy task."

"At this time, we are taking the first initial step,

which is to send fleets to patrol the borders of our system," Renee said. "We know the Queen and the Concords will come. We just don't know when or how."

"What changed?" Hack tilted his head and watched his parents. "What made our system ready to do this?"

"Tammol," Morgan said.

Alois nodded. They both had been on the planet when Water and the Concords took it.

Morgan swallowed hard and held Stardust close to his chest, stroking his little head. "It was so easy for the Concords to slip in and steal a planet. Haven and Burnished Hold don't have strong defenses like some of the others."

"Even Grellweir and Siren's Lament could be taken if the force were large enough and they had no allies," Selene said.

Renee nodded. "You're right. The situation on Tammol frightened a lot of planetary governments in the galaxy. Our system isn't likely to be the only one that bands together."

"For now, Hack, I'm asking each of the generals to ask for volunteers to man the ships going to the Defense Force," Fasi said. "Start asking around, please. It'll be at least another year before we have it up and running, but I want to have a number of volunteers ready."

"Got it," Hack said, nodding.

"This means that we can focus on defeating the Queen and the Concords, doesn't it?" Draif asked. "If we don't have to worry as much about protecting the system, our focus can go to the bigger picture."

"Yes," Renee said, smiling. "We have Cas and the Green fleet searching the galaxy for Air and Fire and collecting any prisoners rescued from Concord ships. Beol's people are using their contacts to hunt them as well. We do know they aren't on Genarg."

"Audre and the Yellow fleet are focused on the Concords," Fasi said. "That leaves Hack and Sheiria's fleets at the station's disposal." He nodded. "That's what we have going on, folks." Ava raised her hand, and Fasi smacked his hand to his face. "I almost forgot. Ava, do you want to tell them?"

She stood and grinned. "Several diplomats from the station have been reaching out to the other mercenary groups. At this moment, ten groups have allied with us against the Concords. They are picking them off, one by one, and sending any rescued prisoners to Cas. He sends them either home or to Tammol." The room cheered. "We are still in talks with five other groups, and things are progressing well."

"What about the Queen?" asked Dannol, Hack's pilot. "Will they fight against her too?"

"Most will," Ava said. "They understand that she is behind the Concords' behavior."

"What will they get out of it?" Dannol asked. "Mercenaries fight for pay."

"They get anything they find on the Concord ships, including the ships," Ava said. "The only exception are the Concords' prisoners." She smiled softly. "To be honest, these ten groups are fighting because of what the Concords are doing to non-human species." She shot Fasi a fond look. "I think our Lord Admiral has inspired his old friends."

Fasi was flustered, the large purple Grell blushing. "Well, that's it for today. Get back to work or back to your time off."

Renee darted straight to Nina. "Hey there, pretty girl," she said and took the baby from Dru. "You're growing like a weed. Yes, you are." She looked at Alois. "How's Sebastian doing?"

"He's recovered and back to work," Alois said happily.

Renee shook her head. "No. I mean has he settled into the station? He's been having a lot of trouble accepting that he's part of our family now. He's also been worried about contributing to Charybdis Station."

"That's stupid," Dru said, frowning. "The man has worked his ass off alongside Leti and Shae. They figured the artifacts out and are still providing us with important information."

"I know that," Renee said. "You know that, and Alois, here, knows that. Sebastian, however, doesn't."

"I didn't know he was struggling so much," Alois said, feeling guilty as hell. "We talked almost every day while I was gone, and he didn't say anything about it." He sighed. "He wouldn't though, would he?"

"No," Renee said. "Work on it, Alois. He's a good man, and our station is better off for having him here. He needs to learn that." She kissed Nina's head and passed her to Alois.

Fasi joined them and hugged his son. Hack's feet

left the ground, and he whined. "Dad, stop. Everyone's watching."

"Oh, Willard," Dru said. "You just hush and give your daddy a hug."

"I hate you, Dru. So much," Hack said.

Fasi just laughed and set his son on his feet. He turned to Alois and draped an arm over his shoulder. "I need to speak with you, Alois." He steered him toward a more secluded spot.

"What's wrong?"

"I don't know for sure," Fasi said. "We spent a couple weeks with Nina and Sebastian." He looked hesitant. "I think you need to talk to him about mates."

"He knows we're mates," Alois said, puzzled.

"I gathered that from your kiss at the spaceport," Fasi said dryly. "I mean, I think you need to explain that being mates doesn't mean you automatically live happily ever after. That takes time, luck, and work."

"What are you talking about?" Alois frowned. Being mates *did* mean you automatically fell in love and lived happily ever after.

Fasi's eyes softened. "Your parents weren't life-mates?"

"No," Alois said and left it at that.

"A life-mate is someone that you are predisposed to connect well with. Sometimes two people just suit each other perfectly. Look at Hack and Leti and then Morgan and Wyatt. It happened fast for both couples, and they settled right in, but that doesn't mean it didn't take understanding and compromises," Fasi said. "The only thing having a life-mate guarantees is a chance. It doesn't guarantee happiness."

Alois was flabbergasted. "A mate won't cheat on you though, right?"

Fasi took his hand. "A life-mate is the person that you're best suited for, Alois, but he or she still has free will. When we were with Sebastian, I got the feeling he thought life-mates were an instant fix-it-all. He was scared to death that you wouldn't be mates, so he didn't understand that his love for you was far more important than that kiss you shared. It may have said you were mates, but it's not what makes him look at you like you've hung the stars."

Alois took a deep breath and thought about Sebastian. Alois loved him before he knew they were mates, not *because* they were mates. He knew he could trust Sebastian not to betray him. Wasn't that just what he'd been thinking a few days ago? This didn't change anything, not really. He let his breath out slowly. Why did it feel like his world had fallen apart?

5

An hour after Alois and Nina left, Sebastian finished translating the last page of the historical account. He shut the book with a *thunk* and sat back in his chair, thinking. His communicator chimed, and he looked at the caller. *Nope,* he thought. He rejected it, then pushed the historical book aside and pulled out his favorite Crellic book. He really should tell Leti about it, but the book was absolutely fascinating. It was a training guide for a beginning Shaman.

The short book highlighted the basics of Crellic Shamanism. He opened it and began at the first page. Again. He'd read it front to back six times since he'd finished translating it, and the book was starting to make sense. Crellic Shamanism was instinctual to begin with. The book hinted at more complex ideas in advanced training, but it claimed the hardest step was the first one – awakening to the spirit world. Not every

Crell was able to do it, and Sebastian wasn't even the right species.

There were symbols to use that helped, but without the intent and the primitive connection between the soul and the galaxy around him, they weren't worth much. He'd drawn them over and over, but nothing ever came of it. He always felt foolish trying. It was one thing to know the Queen was an ancient Crellic shaman and another to really *believe* in the Crells' religious philosophy. As ridiculous as it made him feel, he was starting to believe.

He pushed the book away and closed his eyes, trying to feel it. He'd felt something last time he'd tried. Mustachio hummed in the background. His bird liked to sing and hum, and it helped Sebastian focus. He settled into the hum, sinking into it and searching for the threads of the spirit world the guide mentioned. He stayed like that for a while, searching. He let his mind float, free of worry and logic.

Then he saw it. A thin, silver thread flowed from him to Mustachio. He knew his eyes were shut, but he still saw it. He saw the room around him and the threads joining everything together. The wood of the table and the floors, the metals of the appliances, the green and brown threads of his potted ivy, the magnificent complex beauty of Mustachio. He felt the elements around him, not the Queen's elements, but the elements that built the galaxy.

His fingers moved on the table, tracing the symbols he had memorized months ago – earth, water, air, fire, life, and death. His thread poured from his fingers and into the table, and he heard a sizzle. His eyes flew open, and he stared at the overlapping symbols seared into the table. They were exactly like the symbols on the cover of the book.

"What the fuck?" His voice startled him and Mustachio both. He looked at the bird. "What did I do? How did I do that?"

Sebastian took a breath and tried again. His mind settled faster this time, but Mustachio's humming still helped. He pushed his senses out of the room and moved through the neighborhood, blushing when he touched on Silas and Rune. They weren't just snuggling this time. He moved on quickly and pushed down, moving through the station. The engineering of Charybdis Station was impressive with normal sight. Looking at it through the spirit world made it all the more fascinating. The elements twisted and danced together to create this place, and the engineers led them, minds beyond amazing.

"What are you doing?"

The voice startled him, and he was back in his body again. He turned around in his chair. Dr. Morrick/Death stood in the kitchen doorway. His black eyes were intense and focused squarely on Sebastian.

"Do you know what you're doing, Sebastian?" He was very much Death at that moment.

"Kind of," he said, squeaking. "I translated this beginner's guide to Crellic Shamanism. It's amazing, Dr. Morrick."

"It is," Death agreed. "It's also very dangerous."

"Are you a shaman? I know the Queen is," Sebastian said.

"I'm not," Death said. "Because of our very existence, the Queen's elements cannot practice it. Being around her all the time allowed us to gather quite a bit of knowledge on the topic. Each of us can connect to the spirit world, but that is it."

"I can't believe I did that," Sebastian said, tracing the symbol on the table.

"I can," Death said and sat across from him. "You're very smart and open-minded, and you've been reading Ancient Crellic for months now. The training begins by honing your instinct."

"I'm not that smart," Sebastian said. He watched Death for a minute. "Do you think you could teach me?"

"Why do you want to know?"

"What I saw, all around us, was beautiful and precious," Sebastian said. "At the same time, it was so fragile."

"That's the difference between being a planet and a space station," Death said. "When you open your mind to a planet, it is… I can't even describe the strength."

"I want Charybdis Station to have that," Sebastian said. "I could feel it, and the station wants it too. It wants to live."

"I think that is beyond you and me," Death said softly. "We could make it stronger by protecting it though."

"I can do that," Sebastian said, nodding. He needed to find a purpose and to help Charybdis Station.

"I'll teach you what I can," Death said. "Remember, though, I've never practiced, so I don't know how this will work."

"Why do you want to help? You said it was dangerous, and it's not like I'll learn fast enough to ever compete with the Queen," Sebastian said.

Death picked up the historical book Sebastian had finished that morning. "You read about us, right?"

"Yes," Sebastian said. "You were mostly an ominous presence in the Queen's tower."

He smiled and laughed. "That sounds about right." His smile faded. "Fire is innocent. I don't know how he stayed that way. I don't understand how or why he is the way he is, but I don't want to kill him."

"You want to save him," Sebastian said. "I can't say that I blame you. I've been compiling all the pictures I can find of his collar. It looks like she uses the same binding ritual each time."

"You want to save him too," Death said, smiling again. "You are so much like your cousin, Sebastian."

Sebastian blushed. "I read about all of you. Fire was different. He spent his time racing across the deserts and stole food off people's plates when he visited the villages. He never willingly harmed a single person."

"When the Queen was resurrected, she called us back, giving us our new bodies. We knew immediately that she was different. It broke something in Earth," Death said. "He lost her when they tainted her soul, and he knew it. He became her servant but lost his life-mate. Of course, Life, Air, and Water were ecstatic with the change. She sent them out to terrorize her opponents, and they fucking loved it."

"How did you react?"

"I was indifferent," Death said. "I had always been so numb, so frozen."

"Fire?"

"He was scared," Death said. "He saw what we all did, and he ran. She pulled him back and bound him like a slave. He fought it. Every day, every second that he lived. I know he fights it now."

"We have to help him," Sebastian said, pulling up the pictures of Fire's collar on his tablet.

His communicator chimed, and he frowned at the interruption. He didn't recognize the caller this time. "Um, hello?"

"Sebastian Dolarnio?" A man's face filled the air above the comm.

"Yes?"

"My name is Dr. Advaith Chopra. I'm a professor at a private university on Vextonar."

"Leti's mentioned you," Sebastian said.

"Leti said that you are excellent with languages and are familiar with Vextonian?"

"Yeah," Sebastian said. The language wasn't used anymore since humans had taken over Vextonar and Vextonians were made into second-class citizens. Sebastian had found it fascinating because it was so different from the others he knew, and there were so few people who bothered with it.

"Thank goodness," Dr. Chopra said. "I am in desperate need of a translator for Vextonian. My associate found some beautiful books from Pre-Human Diaspora Vextonar. Can I scan them to you? We'll pay you well for your time, and I'll be sure to recommend you to my colleagues."

"Oh," Sebastian said, surprised. "Sure. Okay. Just send them to me."

"Excellent! Thank you, Mr. Dolarnio."

The man's smiling face disappeared as the call ended, and Sebastian stared at Death. "Did I just get hired to translate for a university professor?"

Death grinned. "You did. I told you that you were smart, didn't I? If Leti is recommending you to his university friends and this man does the same, you'll be in demand in no time."

"Do I have time for that? I have so much to figure out. We have to save Fire," Sebastian said.

Death patted his hand and stood. "You have a mate, don't you? A man you love and trust? Together, you will figure it all out. Plus, I'll be helping you. To start, we'll train and research the binding three days a week. That leaves you four other days to handle translating and me four days to work with Wyatt and Orsla to permanently destroy Life and Water."

"What if it's too much?"

"Then we'll adapt," Death said. "We will make it happen. Congratulations, Sebastian."

Sebastian watched him leave, then stared at Mustachio. "Did all that just happen?"

"Was that Dr. Morrick leaving?" Alois pushed Nina's stroller into the kitchen.

"Yeah," Sebastian said, still dazed. "You're home early. Did everything go alright?"

"I don't know," Alois said, face grim. He must have noticed the stunned look on Sebastian's face. "What's wrong?"

Sebastian summed up his morning, showing him the symbol branded into their table, and told him about the translation work. "Am I crazy? Did I not wake up this morning?"

"Beautiful, you are just fine," Alois said, pulling him into a hug. "The translation work is great. You wanted a new job, and now you have one. The shaman stuff is... scary." Alois leaned his head on top of Sebastian's. "It sounds extremely dangerous."

"It does," Sebastian agreed. "It calls to me though. I feel like I have two paths I could follow. I could be normal and focus on the translating jobs, or I could be a weirdo and become a Crellic Shaman."

Alois snickered. "Weirdo. There's no reason that you can't do both, as much as I hate the thought of you being in the thick of things. If it's what you want, then train with Death. The translation work can build up slowly. Life won't always be so hectic. Hell, in the future, you may decide to get a linguistics degree or something."

"Maybe," Sebastian said. His hands were shaking. He could provide for his family and help Charybdis Station. He shook his head. "What were you going to say before? When you first came in?"

Alois's smile faded. "Fasi told me that life-mates

were just people that were well-suited. You don't have to love me, and you could cheat on me."

"What?" Sebastian sat back in his chair. Alois looked agonized. "Of course, I don't *have* to love you. I love you because of the person you are, not because you're my mate. That's why I'm glad we were separated for so long, even though I missed you. It gave us time to get to know one another." Sebastian grabbed his hand. "Alois, I would never, ever sleep with another person. Hell, I can't even have full sex with you, and the gods know I want to."

"I know that," Alois said. "I do."

"Your head is telling you differently, isn't it?"

"My parents were horrible to each other, Sebastian. They claimed they loved one another, but my dad slept with one of my mom's friends. Then she slept with one of his, and it never ended. It was like a game to see who could hurt who more."

"You thought having a life-mate would keep that from happening to you?"

"Yeah."

"It won't," Sebastian said, and Alois looked up, startled. "Loving *me* will keep that from happening to you." Sebastian bit his lip and laid his head against Alois's chest. "I understand how you feel. I kept telling myself you were stuck with me now. You wouldn't be able to leave when you discovered what a loser I was. I thought mating would be a way to keep you with me always."

"Beautiful, you are not a loser," Alois said. "I don't

like it when you put yourself down, and I'm not going anywhere."

Sebastian smiled. "We both need to trust each other. We need to talk to each other when we start doubting ourselves. We have to be honest and open about how we feel."

"Then that's what we'll do," Alois said. "I love you, Sebastian. I know I never told you that, but I thought it was understood since we're mates. I'll make sure I say it so much you have to believe it."

Sebastian leaned forward and kissed his mate. They would make it work.

6

Sebastian sat on Alois's lap on the couch. They were watching some stupid matchmaking reality show filmed on the planet Elusa in the Radiant System. The planet was a hotbed for celebrities. The beaches looked stunning, but the drama was too much. Sebastian stared at Alois as his mate watched the screen in fascination. Sebastian leaned into him and made a face at the vid-screen. The things he did for his mate.

A knock at the door gave Sebastian the reason he needed to avoid watching the man on the show fall in love with each of the three matches the professionals sent him. "I'll get it," Sebastian said. "You stay here and watch your show. It's time for the guest celebrity appearance. You wouldn't want to miss what advice Irynn Trec'kji gives this guy."

"I know. Irynn is so wise," Alois said. Gods, the man was serious.

Sebastian opened the door, still shaking his head.

All of Leti's kids and Hack's siblings stood on his doorstep dressed in their night clothes. Mo held his rabbit, Abbot, and Pax and Gravy paced behind them. Alex carried a sobbing Sami, and Hack's younger sister, Rose, looked damned scared and carried Pepper.

"What's wrong, guys?" He pulled Rosie in, and she came easily. The others followed.

"Leti's having the baby, and Sami is really frightened because Will fainted. Grandpa Moses told us to bring everyone over here so we don't hear Leti cry. He's in a lot of pain." Rose looked close to tears. "Can we stay here?"

"That would be perfect, Rosie," Sebastian said. "Why don't we put Pepper and Sami to bed. I have a spare crib upstairs I use when I'm watching Wyatt's twins."

"Will Leti be alright?" Alex was pale and worried. Normally, the young man was an over-confident seventeen-year-old, but he adored Leti and Hack.

"He has to be alright," Rose said, lip trembling.

Rizzie yawned and rubbed her eyes. The little girl carried her purple stuffed wolf, Milo, and didn't look a bit worried. "Daddy Leti yelled really loud," she said and patted Rose's leg. "It seems scary now, but it'll be fine. Daddy Leti and Daddy Will are super tough. They'll get the baby out soon. I told Daddy Leti what to name him too."

Sebastian kissed the top of Rizzie's head and wrapped his arm around Rose's shoulders. He led them toward the stairs. "Giving birth hurts like hell, guys, but it's all worth it. Rizzie is right. He'll be just fine."

"Hey," Alois said, climbing the stairs behind them.

"Leti's finally having his baby?" His eyes shifted between Alex, Mo, and Rose's nervous faces. "He'll be so happy to hold his new son in his arms."

"He will," Mo said, swallowing hard.

Alois took Pepper from Rose. "I'll go get this little bit settled and check in on Nina. Alex, can you bring Sami?" Alois headed to the nursery, and Sebastian led a distraught Rose and Mo to one of the guest rooms. Rizzie followed behind, already half asleep. She jumped in the bed as soon as the door opened and burrowed under the blankets.

"Come on, Mo," she said, patting the bed. The boy's smile was small, but there. He crawled into bed, putting Abbott between them.

"I just… Leti has been so great," Rose said quietly. "We've only been here a few weeks, but he's so welcoming. He hugs me and tells me he loves me every day, Sebastian. Every. Day. He means it too."

"He'll be fine, Rose," Sebastian said. "I'll head over there and help out too. I know Nettle and Wyatt will help him through this."

"Women die a lot in childbirth on Burnished Outpost," Rose whispered. "Leti didn't want to go to Medical."

"Trust me. Nettle and Wyatt will bring Medical to him. Rune and Lilah will be there too, and they're both nurses," Sebastian said. "Now, why don't you lie down in the other guest room and get some rest?"

"I don't think I can sleep," she said, following him out the door. "I'm sorry."

"That's actually perfect," Sebastian said. "If you

don't mind, will you keep Alois company? He's watching this stupid reality show, and I can't stand it."

"Stupid?" Alois's outraged voice came from behind him. "Love's Perfect Match is the best show in the galaxy."

Sebastian turned around and patted Alois's cheek. "I'm starting to doubt your maturity level, honey. Sometimes I think you're a wise adult, then I see you with your friends and realize that you have an inner ten-year-old. Now I know you also have an inner sixteen-year-old."

"Come on, Alex and Rosie," Alois said, nose in the air. "I'll show you my show. You'll love it." The two teenagers laughed and followed him down the stairs.

Sebastian watched them settle on the couch and leaned down to give Alois a kiss. "I'll be back after a while." He looked between Alex and Rose. "I'll keep you all updated."

"Thanks," Rose said, then turned to the vid-screen. Her face scrunched up. Yeah, he knew how she felt.

He walked the pebbled path between his and Leti's houses in the dark. Wobble slept in one of the corners, unconcerned with the impending birth of another Hackett.

The door slammed open right when he reached it, and Hack grabbed Sebastian's shoulders. "Leti's having the baby! Fuck, Sebastian, he's hurting."

"That's normal, Hack. Let me in, and we'll go check on him. Are Nettle and Wyatt here yet?"

"Yeah. Rune's helping too."

Sebastian led a passive Hack to the living room.

"Are you sure you won't faint? You're too big for me to catch, Hack."

"I'll be fine," Hack said. "It's just Leti having a baby. Oh, fuck. Leti's having the baby."

Sebastian struggled not to laugh at his panic.

Dru, Beck, and Selene sat in the living room. Sebastian knew the rest of the crew was spread throughout the house and neighborhood.

"It's okay, Hack," Beck said, holding his tail in a death grip. "It's okay."

"Beck is broken," Selene said, voice flat and monotone. "Birth is beautiful, Hack. Beautiful."

"Uh, yeah, what they said." Dru looked almost as bad as Hack. Monty sat on her head and stared at Sebastian.

"Will," Leti yelled from the bedroom upstairs. "Get your ass in here."

Hack stared at Sebastian. "I can't go in there."

Sebastian sighed and tried to push Hack up the stairs. "Guys, help."

Beck, Dru, and Selene worked together and basically carried Hack up the stairs.

"No," Hack said, shaking his head. "I can't see Leti in all that pain. He'll hate me forever. I was the one that got him pregnant."

Grandpa Moses leaned out of the room and grabbed Hack. "Come on, Willard. You'll want to be here for this. Stop being an idiot."

Sebastian didn't bother hiding his laughter and followed Hack into the room. Leti was in the bed, leaning back against Princess. His dragon was curled behind him, vibrating with a loud, rough rumble. Draif sat at one side, holding Leti's hand. His face was pale and sweaty, and Sebastian wondered if they would have two men fainting in here.

Nettle and Wyatt shared the space, checking on Leti while Rune and Lilah kept medical supplies clean and handy. Fasi and Renee sat in a corner, out of the way and holding hands, waiting for their new grandson. Tears already ran down Fasi's cheeks, and Renee didn't look much better. Sebastian went to Shae, and they stood in the corner with Fasi and Renee.

Hack took a deep breath and stood straight. He went to Leti and gripped his other hand. "Damn, baby. You didn't have to yell. I was on my way."

ALOIS TURNED off the vid-screen and grabbed blankets for Alex and Rose. The teenagers were asleep on the couch. Sebastian had been gone for a few hours now and had sent messages and pictures to all the crew and their families to keep them updated. He grabbed the baby monitor and slipped out the front door, jogging to Hack's house. Silas, Remy, and Maia sat on the front steps, looking ragged.

"Why do you three look like you just gave birth?" Alois sat beside the two guards and nodded hello to Remy.

"We're supposed to guard Leti," Maia said. She pointed upstairs. "We can't help with that."

"Nettle and Wyatt gave him some good stuff, so at least he isn't hurting anymore," Silas said.

"Sebastian says the baby will be here soon," Alois said. "Then you'll have another little Hackett to guard."

Maia gave him a dirty look. "Don't remind me."

Remy snickered. "The house gets smaller every day." He nudged Maia with his shoulder. "I'll be moving out at the end of the month."

"You're the easiest to deal with," Maia said. "You should stay and take guard duty for Princess Buttercup."

Remy shuddered. "No thanks. That scary-ass dragon is a softy when it comes to Leti, but I'm not Leti."

"Where are you moving?" Alois knew the young man didn't have a home to go back to. He'd been taken by the Concords while he was at work and tortured for months. No one had reported him missing.

"Shae and I are going to share an apartment a few blocks over," Remy said. "I got a job at Juniper's diner, and Ava managed to locate my cat, Potato. Leti and Hack have been so kind, but I'm ready to stand on my own two feet." He laughed and patted his two new robotic legs. "Coming back from the dead really makes you appreciate life, and I'm ready to live it."

Alois grinned. The kid sure handled coming back from the dead well. "What happened to your cat when you didn't come home?" Alois was sad no one had cared about the sweet man enough to check on him.

"One of my neighbors stole all of my stuff and kicked him outside. Luckily, another neighbor was feeding him. Ava somehow found him, and one of General Caspian's ships picked him up." Remy smiled wide. "I can't wait for him to get here."

"Why did you name him Potato? That's a strange name for a pet," Maia said.

"I love potatoes," Remy said and shrugged. Alois hid a smile.

Sebastian pushed the door open, his smile blinding. "Do you guys want to meet the baby?"

"Hell yeah," Silas said, standing quickly. He helped Remy to his feet.

Alois took Sebastian's hand. "You tired, beautiful?"

"Exhausted," Sebastian answered. "It's so worth it though. He's beautiful, Alois. It makes me want to get pregnant right away."

"We can do that," Alois said, perking up.

Sebastian rolled his eyes. "Come on and see the baby." He tugged him into the living room where all of Blue Solace and their friends were gathered. "Fasi said he'd bring the baby down in a minute. Hack won't leave Leti's side, even though all he's doing is sleeping."

Draif came down the stairs and collapsed on the couch next to Lucas. "That was crazy."

"Do you want kids of your own now, Draif?" Alois asked, eyeing Lucas. The man's eyes were glued to Draif's face.

"Maybe one day, but I'm going to fucking Medical to give birth," Draif said. "Maybe they can just knock me out, then I can wake up and see the baby."

"Doesn't work that way," Morgan said with a grin

and laughed. They all quieted when they heard the bedroom door open.

Fasi walked down the stairs slowly, as if he was afraid he'd drop the little bundle in his arms. The large purple Grell's face was wet, and his smile was damn sweet. He held Leti and Hack's son out for everyone to see. The baby had Hack's dark skin and the tattoos of the Burnished. His hair, though, was all Leti. A little curl of red sat atop his head.

"Hi, everyone," Fasi said. "I'd like you to meet my youngest grandson, Milo Willard Hackett."

7

Alois sat on the floor and watched Nina roll around on her tummy. He couldn't help but smile when she shook her rattle and laughed. She had grown so much in the past two months. It was ridiculous. Sebastian sat on a large purple pillow in the corner, eyes closed and face serene. Dr. Morrick—no, Death sat beside him on his own green pillow. Alois didn't know what the two of them were doing, but he had the day off and a baby to play with.

The light glinted off the lighter streaks in Sebastian's dark hair and warmed his tan skin. Alois sighed, feeling like an idiot as his heart beat faster. His mate did funny things to his insides, but that was as it should be. Nina kicked her feet back and laughed again. Her pink tutu stuck up in the air as she did her best to wiggle forward.

Mustachio hummed and trilled from the open windowsill. The bird was a homebody, but he did occasionally like to fly around the sector. Fortunately, he always came home, and it seemed like he was always present for Sebastian's training.

Sebastian's dark eyes popped open, and he grinned at Alois and Nina. "The two of you are even more beautiful in the spirit world. I could watch you all day."

"Their souls are quite lovely," Death agreed. The element watched as Alois's mate stood and stretched. "Sebastian, you are progressing faster than I thought you would. You've about mastered the basics and have an above average connection to the spirit world. I think we can start working on the next level of training. I remember a rite of passage the Shamans went through at this stage back on Genarg. It will point us toward your element affinities."

Alois grinned, proud of Sebastian. He worked so hard every single day. He was on his third translation job and still translating Ancient Crellic for Leti, as well as training with Death. His mate was damn tenacious. "What are element affinities?" Alois had to admit it all made him curious.

"While a Shaman must master all six elements, he or she will have a more natural connection to two or three," Death said. "During her first life, the Queen had an affinity for earth, water, and air – a simple combination that many underestimated. When she bound us to her, affinities no longer mattered, her power did. She used that power wisely then. Now, of course, she is different." His eyes were sad for a moment, then brightened. "I have an idea of what Sebastian's affinities will be, but we'll do the rite and properly test him."

Sebastian hugged the man, then plucked Nina off the floor. "Sweet girl, are you already trying to crawl? Slow down and stay our baby." He leaned back down and kissed Alois. "I swear she's twice the size she was a month ago." Alois heard his mate's comm chime. Sebastian looked at it, then stuck it back in his pocket. He did that a lot, and Alois had an idea who called him.

Alois stood. "Morrick, we're heading over to Juniper's for dinner. Would you like to join us?"

"I think I'll get home. Ma is visiting with Morgan and Wyatt, so that means there will be good food involved."

Alois snorted. "I understand. They came for dinner here last night." He walked Sebastian's mentor to the door while Sebastian took Nina with him to get ready for dinner. "Sebastian is really progressing fast, right? Will it get more dangerous from here on out?"

Death considered him a moment. "Shamanism isn't dangerous really. What a person does with the power they learn to wield is what's dangerous. I don't think Sebastian will take needless risks, but he will protect others. It's in his nature to do so." He patted Alois's shoulder. "I'll do my best to protect him too, Alois. He is a good man, and there aren't enough of those in this galaxy."

"Thanks," Alois said softly. He smiled wryly. "I think I'll always worry."

"That's not a bad thing," Death said and left, walking slowly down the street toward Morgan and Wyatt's house. Trixie stuck her head through the fence and bleated loudly as Death walked past her. Alois smiled as the man pulled a treat out of his pocket and fed her before continuing on.

"Are you ready?" Sebastian stood behind Alois, and Nina was already in her stroller. Mustachio took off out the window for his late afternoon tour of the neighborhood.

"Yeah," Alois said, taking his hand and heading down the street. They didn't make it far before his comm sounded. He checked it. "Fuck. There's an emergency meeting with the Lord Admiral."

"Oh no," Sebastian said. "That's never a good thing. I'll take Nina on to Leti's. He'll want the company if Hack has to leave."

"I'm sorry, beautiful," Alois said, sad that he'd miss spending an evening with his mate.

"It's an emergency," Sebastian said, kissing him. "Go on and keep me updated." He grinned. "This gives me a chance to steal Milo from Leti for a little bit."

Alois laughed. Leti, Hack, and their kids doted on the newest Hackett. It was hard to get some cuddle time with the boy. Alois headed toward the tram, then Sebastian turned and headed toward Leti's. Alois tried not to pout.

"Damn, that's a pretty pout," Cordelia said, linking her arm with his as she headed toward the tram too.

"I *am* pretty," Alois said, sniffing.

They arrived along with the rest of the Blue Solace crew and the other officers in Hack's fleet. Alois sat between Dru and Cordelia, watching the large conference room fill up.

Fasi and Renee came in together. They both looked

tired. "I'm sorry for the short notice," the Lord Admiral said. He sighed heavily and stood at the front of the room. "We were sent two very important pieces of news today, one from Cas and one from Half-Moon Guild Master Beol." He looked to Renee.

She cleared her throat and typed onto her tablet. The picture of a man projected above them. He was an older human with white hair and a wrinkled face. His eyes were completely white. They looked like creepy, swirling clouds.

"First, Cas found Air's last location. The element has been on a small luxury vacation planet in the Boral System, Bredell. The planet is tiny and privately owned. It consists of Spa Lodges for tourists and housing for the employees of the Lodges. Communications have been cut off from the planet for the past three months, but not many were notified since the planet is so off-track and provides its guests with complete seclusion. Cas landed yesterday, and the planet is absolutely devastated."

"According to the few survivors, Air and a small group of Concord mercenaries landed three months ago. The Concords blocked all off-world communications, and Air began to ravage the planet with storms," Fasi said, eyes tired and sad. "No location was spared. There are only a handful of survivors."

"Families of Bredell's guests rallied and hired a mercenary ship to go check on the planet. That's how Cas heard of the trouble," Renee said. "He left to check it out. Air was gone by the time he arrived, but just barely. Beol and a team are tracking him now. We sent this picture of Air to the media, but everyone is a bit skeptical."

"Bad weather destroyed the whole planet?" One of Hack's captains asked doubtfully.

"It was a bit more than bad weather," Fasi said, voice hard. "The planet is half the size of Charybdis. As soon as Air landed, there were suddenly six hurricanes and countless tornadoes and typhoons."

Alois and Cordelia exchanged horrified looks.

"This kept up for a full three months," Renee said. "There is barely a building left standing."

"Fuck," Hack said. "What can we do?" His dog Gravy sat at his feet, and Hack played with his ears, worry clear in his eyes.

"I'm meeting with the leaders of our system today," Fasi said. "We'll send as much aid as we can. I've notified my contacts in the other systems, and they'll do what they can. Cas spoke with our closest ally, the Belcrest Mercenary group. They're sending ships to take over the search for other survivors so Cas can get back to work."

"Beol is tracking Air?" Draif asked.

"Yes," Renee said. "He has his trail now and will find him."

"What about the rest of the Half-Moon?" Morgan asked. Stardust was looking a little bigger today and stretched out on his back along Morgan's shoulder, showing off the blue scales of his belly.

"There is still a unit in the Crellic System, acting as our eyes," Fasi said. "Wolfe is bringing the remaining members and their families here from Union Station. They will be here in a few months."

"That brings us to our second bit of news. Beol's people located Fire," Renee said. "They've been watching a large fleet of Concords gathering around Genarg for a couple of months now. Cas and Audre noticed more movement than normal in their systems."

"Fire left on the Concord Admiral's flagship yesterday," Fasi said. "Beol's people did some snooping, and one assassin stowed away on the flagship. She discovered that the remaining Concords, led by Fire and Admiral Sharp, are on the way to us. They want to bring Death back to the Queen, as well as Water and Life's artifacts."

"What size fleet are we talking about?" Hack asked. Alois could see the gears already turning in the Blue General's head.

"Three times the size of ours," Fasi said. "That's including all four of our fleets and our personal defense."

"That must be every last Concord ship out there," Selene said, voice as emotionless as usual. "This could be fun." Everyone in the room turned to stare at her. She stared back, face blank. "If we win, they're wiped out. No more Concords."

"We have half of our fleet here," Hack said, thoughtfully. "Cas and Audre are out and about. Hmm."

"Beol's men are still tracking them," Draif added. "The fleet can't possibly stop for fuel and supplies all together."

Hack smiled. "Unfortunate attacks happen all the time in spaceports."

"Might be a little scuffle with Audre or Cas," Draif said. "Maybe a sneaky assassin gets on board a ship and sabotages the engines."

Renee gave them an approving look. "Cas, Audre, and Beol's people could chip away at the fleet and give us a better chance."

"What about Concord prisoners on board their ships?" one of Hack's captains asked. "We still need to save them."

"Yes," Fasi agreed. "That will determine our strategy."

"Luckily, we have Dr. Morrick," Hack said, gesturing to the corner, and Alois looked behind them. Death sat by himself in the shadows.

"I can freeze the ships and harvest the souls of the Concords," Death said. "Then you all could go aboard and free any prisoners."

"Ideally, that would work just fine. It might be time consuming, but it means very few casualties, if any, on our side," Draif said. "However, that's not taking Fire into account."

"I can't freeze him for long," Death said. "He is constantly moving, and it's like holding a wiggling eel with your bare hands."

"What can he do from a ship?" Selene asked.

"Beol's people provided us some information about that as well," Fasi said. "The spy onboard the flagship saw him in action. For some reason, he lost his temper and destroyed about a third of the engines in their small fighter vessels. They just exploded. The ships had to be towed back to Genarg."

"There are a million ways a ship can spark and ignite," Death said. "He could easily take out our entire fleet." The room grew quiet, and Alois exchanged hopeless looks with Dru and Cordelia.

"What chance do we stand?" Fasi asked, sitting.

Death's smile was startling. "He is fighting the Queen's control. As unlikely as it sounds, Fire doesn't have a short temper. He doesn't really have any temper. He is fighting for control of himself."

"He didn't get mad and accidently kill some fighters," Renee said thoughtfully. "He purposefully took a shot while he could."

"How can that help us?" Draif asked. "His intentions can be all kinds of good, but if the Queen controls him, we don't stand a chance."

Death shot Alois a look and winced. "Alois won't like this idea, but Sebastian and I have a solution."

Alois groaned. "No. Absolutely not."

"One ship goes to meet Fire and his fleet," Death said. "They want me alive."

"No, no, no," Alois said. Gravy whined and climbed to his feet. The large dog walked a few chairs over and stuck his head under Alois's arm, pressing his big body against his side in comfort.

"Sebastian and a small number of others will go with me to Fire's ship. While I'm distracting Fire and the admiral, Sebastian can undo the binding collar on Fire," Death said.

Alois's head fell to the side, landing on Dru's

shoulder. Monty barely avoided being squashed. He glared at Alois and crawled to the top of Dru's head. Alois petted Gravy's head and tried not to yell and scream.

"Sebastian can do that?" Renee looked shocked. She looked at Fasi. "Our Sebastian?"

"He's damn smart, but how is that possible?" Fasi asked.

"He found a training guide for Crellic Shamanism," Death said. "He started on the path as soon as he finished translating it. I felt him awaken to the spirit world, and I've been training him. Together, we've also been studying the binding collar from pictures and videos from previous cycles. Sebastian has a way with working out puzzles. We've almost figured it out."

"He's my mate," Alois said, eyes pleading with Death. "He is everything to me. There's no living without him at my side. Please find another way."

"I'm sorry, Alois," Death said. Alois knew he was. He'd gotten to know both Death and Morrick better over the last couple of months. The man adored Sebastian. "I can't unbind Fire myself. I'm an element, as twisted and bound to life as I am, I cannot act as a Shaman. I can see and feel the spirit world, and I know the training and spells, but I can't actually do them." He stood and walked to Alois. "I *can* promise you that I will protect Sebastian with my last breath."

"I don't like it," Fasi said, shaking his head. "Sebastian isn't a trained fighter."

"Trained or not, he *is* a fighter," Hack said. "He stood with us against the Concords and tried to protect

Dr. Morrick and Death's artifact. He has determination, cleverness, and apparently Shaman skills. Shamanism skills? Shaman powers? Shamanistic magic? Something like that."

"How do we know that's even a thing?" Nettle shrugged. He was a doctor and a man of science, so Alois understood where he was coming from. "I don't want to piss you off, Death, but magic? Really?"

"Grell shapeshift," Beck said, shrugging. "Mates have an instant connection. Sirens have mental abilities that confuse the fuck out of everyone else. There's a whole bunch out there that we don't get, Nettle." The big Grell held his tail in his hand, nervously running his fingers over it.

"Can Sebastian give us a demonstration of some kind?" Fasi asked. "I would feel better about this if I knew he could defend himself somehow."

Alois opened his comm and sent Sebastian a message. He waited for the reply, then nodded to Fasi. "He's on his way."

"Let's say he frees Fire," Hack said. "What then?"

"Then I freeze the ships and harvest the Concord souls," Death said. "You and your fleet rescue the prisoners."

"Fire won't attack you as himself?" Cordelia's voice was strained. She reached out and squeezed Alois's hand.

"I don't think so," Death said.

"You don't *think* so? I'm not comfortable with that answer, Morrick," Alois said.

"I will kill Fire myself before I let him harm

Sebastian," Death said. "I want to save my brother, but I won't sacrifice Sebastian to do it."

"Can you bring him back to life if he dies?" Hack asked, and Alois looked up. Leti hadn't found much in the histories to indicate that Death could resurrect people, but their friend Remy was proof that it was possible.

Death sighed. "No. In general, even I cannot stop death or reverse it. The only exception is when I'm looking for a host. I wish it was different," he said. "Wyatt lost some good friends on Tammol, and I would have brought them all back in a heartbeat if I could."

"Okay," Hack said. "I'm sorry to bring it up. I was just thinking of Remy."

"When my essence enters a dead body, one of two things happen. One, the soul has moved on. If that's the case, the body is awakened, but becomes a soulless creature."

"I'd rather that not happen," Alois said. "From what I hear, enforcement had a lot of trouble with that woman when Dr. Franklin used your element to bring her back that way."

Death nodded at him. "The second possibility is that the soul still lingers and desires life, so I merge with it if it is suitable. If it is not, like Remy, I abandon it. Once it is done, though, it is done."

"Why couldn't you bring someone back, then leave them to go back into Morrick?" Alois felt bad for asking, but he was damn curious about Death's abilities. He'd been quiet on the topic, and no one wanted to press him.

"I can't enter a body twice," Death said. "Since we have merged, if I left him, Morrick would be dead for good, and my new host would be stuck with me. Sebastian wouldn't just be Sebastian anymore." He looked sad. "I *am* Morrick, and I don't want to leave Wyatt and the twins behind." He looked around the room. "I'm sorry. The Queen once tried to use this as a weapon, and I traveled from corpse to corpse. It got messy, fast." He somehow managed to look even paler. "What happened was truly sickening."

They continued to debate the plan for another fifteen minutes before Sebastian arrived. He carried Nina in his arms and had her bag slung over his shoulder. He went straight to Alois and cuddled into him. "What's going on?"

Alois held him close and breathed in his scent. He couldn't lose Sebastian, but he knew what Sebastian would choose to do. "Fire is on the way with a Concord fleet," Alois said and quickly summed things up. "I don't want you to go, Sebastian."

8

Sebastian hugged Alois tightly. "Free Fire on my own? Can I even do that?" He spoke softly, watching Alois's face. Sebastian wasn't some well-trained soldier. He was just Sebastian.

Alois winced. "Fuck, fuck, fuck. Sebastian, I know you can do this. I don't want you to, but if anyone can rescue Fire, it's you."

Sebastian rubbed his forehead into Alois's shoulder. He could do it. Right? What choice did he really have? "How many will die if I don't go, Alois?" he whispered. "If Fire and Death battle, the Concord fleet will have plenty of time to destroy our ships, no matter how fast Death is able to defeat him."

"If you go, I go with you," Alois said. "That's not up for debate."

"What about Nina?" Sebastian didn't want Alois to die, period, but what would their little girl do if they both died?

"Cordelia will take her in," Alois said without any hesitation. "Leti would too."

"I will, Sebastian," Cordelia said. "If the worst was to happen and you both died and I survived, I would take care of your daughter." Her eyes glistened. "That shit better not happen though. I'm not ready to be a mom."

"Any of us would take care of her," Dru said. "Fuck. We'd have to fight Ma and Pops for her."

"Grandpa Moses too," Hack said.

"We take care of our own, Sebastian," Fasi said, eyes softening as he came to stand beside them. He stroked Nina's head, then hugged Alois and Sebastian together. "Haven't you figured out you're ours?"

"Damn it," Sebastian said, tears filling his eyes. "People are staring, Fasi."

"Just hush and give your daddy a hug," Hack said with a snort.

Fasi hugged them for a minute longer, then released them. "Okay. Dr. Morrick, how do you suggest we do this demonstration?"

"Sebastian, if you don't mind, we'll do the rite of passage I mentioned earlier. It is meant to be completed in front of your community, so this is convenient."

"Okay," Sebastian said, shrugging. "You didn't tell me what it was though." He passed Nina to Cordelia and got one more kiss from his mate. "Will it work to convince them I'm not just crazy?"

"Yes," Death said. "It's a bit showy. Take off your shirt please." He turned to the room. "I need something to represent each element. Please look around you or through your pockets."

Sebastian followed him to the front of the room as everyone patted themselves down. They found a bottle of water to represent water, the large potted fern from the corner of the room for earth, a whistle from someone's pocket for air, a dead bug from outside for death, and Gravy for life. They placed each item in a circle on the large conference table. Gravy woofed softly when Alois lifted him up and set him down. Sebastian giggled when Alois lifted him up next.

"Fire?" Sebastian looked around. What would work for fire? His hands settled across his soft stomach. He still had a bit of the weight from carrying Nina, and everyone in the room was staring at him.

"I got you," Hack said, stripping off his shirt. He hopped up on the table and sat cross-legged in the spot for fire. He pulled a flame into the palm of his hand and held it up. "Here you go."

"Thanks, Hack," Sebastian said with a grin. "Why did you take your shirt off?"

Hack grinned. "So, you aren't the only half-naked one on the table."

Sebastian snorted, then looked to Death. "Okay, so what do I do?" He really hoped he didn't have to touch the dead bug.

"First, give each element intention, then stand in the middle," Death said.

Fuck. Sebastian had to touch the dead bug. Before he could continue, the door opened and one of Fasi's assistants poked his head in.

"Umm, Lord Admiral, sir," the young woman said nervously. "There's a bird outside the door. I think he wants in."

Fasi looked at Renee. "Remember when sentences like that were just crazy?"

"Let it in, please," Renee told the assistant with a laugh. The assistant opened the door, and Mustachio flew in, settling on the back of Alois's chair.

"Aww, hey, darling boy," Sebastian said. "You're here for emotional support, aren't you?" He walked around the circle, touching each object, animal, or person to give them intention. They would represent each element.

The bird lightly pecked Alois's head. "Yeah," Alois said. "That's what he's here for."

"Alright. Sebastian, settle in the middle of the circle and center yourself," Death said.

Mustachio hummed his song, helping Sebastian settle into the spirit world more quickly. The room was full of threads – each individual, the relationships between them, the hopes and sorrows of each. The bonds forged between Hack's crew were beautiful. Hack himself was linked to Beck and Selene with threads of steel that glowed and twisted, shaping into an unbreakable bond. Fasi and Renee were simply gorgeous. They didn't have one bond, but a thousand linking them together.

It was beautiful and heartbreaking all at once. One of Hack's captains, Sebastian didn't know his name, had just lost his wife. Sebastian could see his grief and see her spirit trying to comfort him. Draif was haunted by his past, his threads darkened and hesitant despite the confidence he displayed. Sebastian bit his lip, wanting to help but uncertain how to do it.

"Now, focus on the six elements around you," Death said, his voice focused and powerful.

Sebastian focused on the six colorful threads leading from the elements into his body. They hummed, growing louder than Mustachio. The rich brown and green thread between Sebastian and earth solidified, growing larger and larger as each second passed. The potted fern slid across the table, stopping to Sebastian's left. The plant was warm against his side, and the fronds tickled his nose.

"What the fuck?" Sebastian barely heard Dru's words as the humming grew louder.

The green and gold thread between Sebastian and life swelled and sang joyfully. It was hard to reconcile such purity and happiness with the Queen's element, Life. The thread expanded, becoming huge, then Gravy slid across the table with a whine. He came to stop at Sebastian's right side. He licked Sebastian's face, then settled his head onto Sebastian's shoulder. The threads quieted for a moment, but Sebastian knew they weren't finished.

"His affinities are Life and Earth? That's not too bad," Alois said. "Gravy knows he isn't a lapdog, right?" Gravy did, in fact, *not* know that. He sat across Sebastian's lap as the hum grew loud again.

"It's not over yet," Death said.

The fiery red and gold thread between Sebastian and fire began to dance. It twirled and brightened as it grew. The blazing thread grew thicker, and Sebastian could barely hear anything over the roar of the flames.

"Damn it," Hack said.

Sebastian grinned. He had definitely heard that. Hack slid across the table, coming to rest against Sebastian's back.

"It had to be Fire," Hack said plaintively.

The three threads encircled him, twisting and entangling with one another. They hummed louder, and Sebastian vaguely heard gasps around the room. He knew what they saw. The spirit world was full of light, welcoming a new shaman. He knew the threads could be seen by all as they snaked around him. They sunk into his skin, and he felt a searing pain on his chest, stomach, and back. "Ouchie!"

"Sebastian," Alois cried. Sebastian felt Death hold his mate back so he wouldn't jump on the table. As fast as the pain appeared, it disappeared. Sebastian opened his eyes, blinking slowly.

Cordelia snickered. "Ouchie? He's such a tough, brave shaman."

"Holy moly, that looks awesome," Dannol said. The pilot's eyes were wide as he stared at Sebastian.

Sebastian looked down. Brown and green threads swirled across the tan skin of his left pectoral muscles. They spread over his shoulder, morphing into a delicate fern frond. He looked to his right and the green and gold threads gathered there. They shifted into a big paw print on his right shoulder. He smiled at it. That was the cutest tattoo ever.

His smile disappeared fast. He looked down and

breathed a sigh of relief. Feathers fanned out across his stomach, arching over his navel. They matched Mustachio's tail feathers perfectly. He poked them. So pretty.

Then he noticed red and gold threads wrapping around his waist from behind. He jumped up, dislodging Gravy and Hack. He tried to look over his shoulder but only ended up spinning in a circle. "Please tell me Hack's face isn't tattooed on my back. Please!"

Hack looked disgruntled. "Whoa there. First, a tattoo of my face would be quite tasteful. Second, you should be so lucky."

"It's alright, beautiful," Alois said, laughing. He reached out and grabbed his leg to stop his circles. "It's a red and gold miniature copy of Hack's tattoo pattern. It's right in the center of your back with threads pouring out from it."

"Oh, thank the gods," Sebastian said, hopping into Alois's arms. Hack's tattoos were thick, jagged lines patterned all over his body. "I really didn't want to explain to Leti why I have his husband's face tattooed on my back."

"Why are Mustachio's feathers on his stomach?" Renee asked.

Death shrugged. "I don't know. The rite of passage is a bit different for everyone."

Sebastian didn't feel any different. He pulled his shirt back on and took Nina back from Cordelia.

"Please tell him that he needs to let me go." A woman's voice came from behind him. He turned around. The captain's wife stood behind him. She glowed brightly and shimmered with silver light. "I'm sorry to bother you, but you two are the only ones who can hear me."

Sebastian looked to Death, who looked uncomfortable. "I've learned that getting involved in matters like this can be complicated. I can see spirits, but I don't know what to do to offer comfort and closure. Many of the Crellic shamans were very good at helping them cross over." Death winced. "They tend to stay away from me in any case."

"Why? I would think they would want your help," Sebastian said.

"What's going on?" Alois and the others looked between Death and Sebastian.

"He can eat spirits like me," the woman said. She watched Death, face sad. "I learned a long time ago that just because someone can do something, doesn't mean they should."

"I don't," Death said quietly. "I never have." He patted Sebastian on the back. "You won't likely see many, but if you want to help those you can see, good luck."

"Thanks," he said wryly. He looked around. Everyone was staring at them. He leaned close to Death.

"It'll just take a moment," she said. "I'm not upset that I'm dead. I'm just really worried about my husband."

"I'll try to help," Sebastian told the woman. "He may not want to hear it though."

"Please. He's a good man, but I can't stand his pain," she said.

Sebastian ignored the strange looks and walked over to the bereaved captain. "Sir, can I talk to you outside for a moment?"

The man looked startled. "Uh, I guess." He looked to Hack, and the general shrugged. Sebastian took him outside the room while Alois and the others started talking strategy again.

"So. This is going to be really weird, but shamans see the spirit world, right?"

"Okay?" The man looked confused.

"We can see a lot about a person too, when we look at them through the spirit world," Sebastian said. "I noticed when I first started the rite of passage that you had lost your wife and you were sad about it."

The man's face grew hard. "That's not any of your business. Of course, I'm upset about losing her."

"I get it," Sebastian said. "You loved her a lot. I see that in your threads. The problem is, her spirit is lingering around you because of your grief."

"What?" The man looked angry now. "Why would you say that?"

"Because it's true?" Sebastian sighed and cuddled Nina close. "Look, I don't know what to say here."

"Tell him that he needs to move on," the woman said.

"Uh, well, she says you should move on," Sebastian said with a wince.

"She died a little less than a month ago," the man said. "How the fuck do I move on right now?"

"Wow," Sebastian said, looking back at the spirit. "A month isn't a long time."

"I can't stand to see him hurt," she said, ghostly face shimmering with tears.

"Maybe not, but he needs time to get used to not having you. If Alois died, it would take me a hell of a lot more than a month to move on. I think he needs some time to grieve," Sebastian told her.

She stomped her foot. "He should move on and find happiness again. I *need* my love to be happy." She frowned. "Just not with Jessica."

"Okay," he said, turning back to the man. "She said you should move on, but not with Jessica."

The man snorted. "Of course, she would say that. She's so damn bossy. Tell her I don't *want* to jump in bed with anyone right now. Damn it! Can I at least have a year?"

Sebastian gave her a look, hand on his hip. "Give the man some time."

"Fine," she said, huffing. "Will you tell him to at least not mope about alone at home?"

"Okay," Sebastian said. "She said she'll back off, but you can't mope all alone at home."

"Damn woman," the man said, throwing his hands in the air. "What does she want from me?"

"He needs friends," she said. "Most of his are on other planets, or in other sectors on Charybdis. Neither of us had any family. Do you?"

"I have my chosen family," Sebastian said. He thought of Sai and Salla. He wouldn't even recognize them anymore. He turned to the man. "She says you need friends," Sebastian said and pulled out his comm, calling quickly.

Leti's figure popped up. He sat in a comfy chair in front of his office vid screen. Sami sat in his lap and a bowl of popcorn was on the desk in front of him. "Sebastian," he said. "Why is Will messaging me about how a tattoo of his face on your back would be amazing, not scary?"

"I'll explain later," Sebastian said. "I need you." He moved to stand beside the man. "This is… Wait, what is your name?"

"Haroon," the man answered.

"This is Haroon," Sebastian said. "Haroon's wife, uh, what was your name?" Sebastian looked at the spirit.

"Elin."

"Haroon's wife, Elin, wants him to have more friends since she's dead," Sebastian said.

Leti stared at him. "Elin is there? Right next to you?" Sebastian nodded. "Sebastian, I love you and believe in you, but this shit is weird."

"Seriously," Haroon grumbled.

Leti turned to him. "Don't you worry, Haroon. I have you now. We have a weekly dinner at my house, and I'm home almost every day. Where do you live? I'll bring the kids by for a visit tomorrow. Do you like llamas? What about Fire Veil Dragons?" He paused, eyes filling with tears. "I'm so sorry about your wife. Oh, I need to hug you so bad right now." He held his arms out to the man. "I'm hugging you with my mind right now, Haroon."

Sami scrunched up his face and held his arms out too. "Me too! Me too!"

Sebastian turned to Elin. "There. He's met Leti and *no one* gets away from Leti. He'll have more friends than he could possibly want soon enough."

Elin smiled. "Good. I guess he does need some time to adjust. Just remind him he can never sleep with Jessica. The bitch doesn't deserve him, but I know she'll be all over him."

"Okay," Sebastian said. "I vow I will make sure he never, ever sleeps with Jessica."

Leti smothered his laughter, and Haroon rolled his eyes. Elin smiled one more time, then disappeared.

"So, I think she's gone." Sebastian looked around. "For now." He pushed Haroon's shoulder. "Who the hell is Jessica? You can't sleep with her, okay? I promised."

9

*A*lois and Sebastian settled Nina into bed, then went to their room. Alois grabbed Sebastian's hand and tugged him into his arms. "The idea of you getting hurt is destroying me," Alois said. He cupped Sebastian's cheek and felt himself sink into his mate's dark eyes. "Despite that, I'm so damn proud of you for stepping up. I know you can do this, and I'll be there right beside you."

Sebastian's tentative smile about broke Alois's heart. He knew his mate still felt like he had to prove himself to Alois and everyone else. He kissed Sebastian, trying to chase his doubts away. Sebastian wrapped his arms around Alois's neck and leaned into him. Alois savored the feel of Sebastian in his arms and the taste of his lips. He loved him so fucking much.

"Alois." Sebastian leaned back and looked up at him. "Can we try again? I think I may be ready this time."

"Anytime, beautiful," Alois said, chuckling. "Anytime

I can have you in my arms, whether my dick ends up in your ass or not, is a damn good time."

"You're so romantic," Sebastian said dryly. He laughed when Alois picked him up and spun him around in circles.

"I do have a way with words," Alois said, tossing him on the bed. He lay down beside his giggling mate and kissed him slowly, running his hands over Sebastian's body. Sebastian's tattoos were beautiful. He swore they moved, twisting and swirling, when he looked at them from the corner of his eye. He hummed with happiness when his own scales settled against the colorful beauty. He nuzzled his face against Sebastian's neck and stroked his mate's dick. "I swear when you're in my arms, everything else just disappears."

Sebastian arched his hips up and spread his legs wide. He ran his hands through Alois's hair. "Me too. I'm safe with you. Everything's better when you're with me."

Alois tentatively stretched Sebastian's slick hole. Sebastian's Wello blood ensured his body would welcome his mate. This was usually where they had to stop. Alois watched Sebastian carefully for any signs of stress or upset, but his mate just watched him with heavy eyes.

When he was stretched, Alois positioned himself and slowly entered his mate. Sebastian moaned and lifted his hips, so Alois held Sebastian's legs up, wrapping them around his waist.

"Alois," Sebastian said softly. "It's you."

"It's me," Alois said with a smile, leaning down to kiss him.

"I wish it had always been you," Sebastian said.

"I'm here now," he said. "It will always be me and you. *Always*."

He started moving, and Sebastian's legs tightened around his waist. They moved together, eyes focused on one another's faces. Alois increased his speed, breathing heavily at the tightness around his dick. Sebastian's hips rose with every thrust Alois made, and it didn't take long for them to reach their peaks. When Alois came, he filled Sebastian and felt Sebastian's cum splatter against his stomach. They both panted, and Alois fell to Sebastian's side, turning him in his arms.

"Damn, beautiful."

"Alois," Sebastian said. "Alois, Alois, Alois."

"Yes?" He smiled down at his mate.

"My head was full of you," Sebastian said. "Not *them*."

"I'm glad," Alois said. He stroked the hair back from Sebastian's face. "Never hesitate to tell me to stop, beautiful. It would kill me if you just tried to struggle through."

"I will," Sebastian whispered, yawning. He snuggled against Alois and was asleep in seconds, still sweaty and sticky. Alois couldn't make himself move. They would be sweaty and sticky together.

THE NEXT MORNING, Alois whistled as he left the tram at the training grounds for Blue Sector.

Morgan fell into step beside him, covering his yawn. "Why the fuck are *you* so happy? Damn, I hate mornings."

"Life is great," Alois said, shrugging. "I can't help it that you're getting as grumpy as Hack."

Morgan gasped. "Take that back."

"*Never*," Alois said, using his best villain voice. He laughed at the look Morgan gave him. "Where's Stardust?"

"Princess Buttercup came to my house, Alois. The fucking dragon came to my house and stared in through my window. When I opened the door, Stardust jumped on his back. They headed down the street toward Leti's," Morgan said, looking horrified. "This is my life now."

Alois laughed hard, then spotted a figure a little way in front of them. "Haroon! Hey, man. Sebastian said I have to be your friend now."

Haroon sighed and waited for them to catch up. "I swear I should have known Elin would find some way to nag the hell out of me, even after death."

Alois laughed, but he could see the grief in the man's eyes. He could act as annoyed as he wanted, but he still missed his wife.

"Lieutenant Destenar." A man walked towards them with two other men. Alois thought he might be one of the pilots for a battle cruiser in Hack's fleet.

"Hey," Alois said, startled by the sound of his last name. No one ever called him by it. Not even Fasi.

The man smirked, setting Alois's teeth on edge. "I didn't realize until last night that you've taken up with that guy from Union Station." He leaned forward, doing his damnedest to look empathetic. "I don't think you know what you've gotten into. Literally." His friends smothered their laughter.

"Be careful here," Alois warned, anger churning in his stomach. He knew where this asshole was going, and he could at least tell Hack he had warned the fucker.

"He's a whore, man," the pilot said. "I fucked him back on Union Station. My buddies here did too. You've seen where he lives, right? He's probably fucking a bunch of guys here to afford that place." The man shrugged, completely oblivious to the danger he was in. "A guy like you has a reputation to maintain. Fuck, I've heard you'll be a captain soon enough. You should drop the whore before others notice, especially since he comes with a bastard."

"He wasn't even a good fuck," one of his friends said, laughing. "He just laid there."

Alois went for the pilot first. Two hits and the guy was on the ground, unconscious. He turned to the other two, then stopped. Haroon had taken one out and Morgan the other. "That was too damn fast," Alois said, growling. He was so damn pissed. "I need something else to hit."

"No," Haroon said, grabbing his shoulder. "You need to calm down. General Hackett is coming, and you need to have a clear head."

"That may not be possible," Morgan said. He kicked his guy in the stomach when he started to get up.

"What the hell, guys?" Hack looked furious. "Fighting? Seriously?"

"I'm sorry if you're upset, sir," Haroon began, standing to attention. "However, these men deserved it."

Hack paused, looking between them. "What happened?"

"These men, uh, knew Sebastian from Union Station and thought they'd enlighten Alois," Morgan said.

Haroon scowled. "They were assholes."

"Oh," Hack said, then shrugged. "Alright then."

The pilot moaned and opened his eyes, seeing Hack. "General Hackett!" He sat up. "Lieutenant Destenar attacked us."

"You shouldn't have called his mate a whore," Morgan said.

"You called him a whore?" Hack looked like he wanted to murder the man. His fire filled his eyes. "You stupid son of a bitch. Did you actually pay a man for the chance to rape Sebastian and now you're calling him a whore?" Hack growled.

"Rape? He's a whore," the pilot said. "There was no rape."

"Did he consent? Did he even look like he wanted to be there?" Haroon looked enraged.

Alois wished he could add his own angry words, but his voice was broken. His poor Sebastian. It was one thing to know something happened, and another to be confronted with the men who hurt his mate. He wanted to fucking kill them.

"He… he didn't say no," the pilot said, standing to his feet. "His boss said it was all legal because he had the right to sell him."

Hack shook his head. "I'm ashamed of you three. It doesn't matter what someone says is legal if it's clearly morally wrong. He didn't want to be there. He didn't agree to be there. He was sold by his shitty parents." He looked behind him. "Finn, will you get these three off my training grounds. I don't know what to do with the assholes, and Alois may try to kill them." He snarled. "*I may try to fucking kill them.*"

Finn and a couple of other guys took the three men away, and Alois could finally breathe.

Hack came to stand next to him. "You alright there, buddy? Your eyes could be phasers right now."

"Fine," Alois bit out.

"Go on home," Hack said. "Hold Sebastian and deal with this." Alois spun on his heels and headed back to the tram. He needed Sebastian.

Sebastian met him at the door, puzzled. "Hack sent me a message saying you needed serious hugs. What's wrong?"

Alois pulled Sebastian into his arms, lifting him off his feet, and buried his face against Sebastian's neck. Alois kissed him, then carried him into the house before setting him back on his feet in the entryway.

"When I was fourteen," Alois said. "My dad came home from work one day, furious. Mom had asked him for money to buy something, I don't remember what.

He didn't give it her. Anyway, he came home that day and started yelling at her. She just sat at the kitchen table and smiled. He said two of the guys he worked with told him she was offering to sleep with men in the neighborhood for money."

"Alois." Sebastian's face lost all color. "Why didn't you say anything before? My past..."

"No," Alois said. "You didn't choose to be there, Sebastian. You were a victim, and I could never hold that against you." Sebastian hugged him tightly, and Alois pressed his face into his dark hair. "By the time my dad figured it out, she had already earned enough money to buy whatever it was she wanted." Alois cupped Sebastian's face. "When I said my parents were horrible to each other, I meant it. They're still married, and they're still making each other miserable. I never thought I could trust anyone that wasn't my mate. My parents sure as shit weren't the only fucked-up couple I ever saw."

"I would never–" Sebastian started to say.

"No explanations needed," Alois said, covering his mate's mouth with his fingers. "When Fasi told me mates weren't somehow magically beholden to never cheat on one another, I was worried that I'd lose you. I was afraid I'd let my fucked-up head get the better of me. I never once doubted you would remain loyal to me."

"Oh, Alois," Sebastian said. "You're it for me. No one else could possibly do now. It's good to hear that you believed in me though."

Alois smiled and kissed him softly. "I'm going to tell

you something, but it's just to make you aware. It's not a problem, alright?"

"Okay?"

"Three guys confronted me at work today," Alois said. "They were some of the men that hurt you on Union Station."

Sebastian turned pale, then flushed red. "No, no, no. Not here."

"Morgan, Haroon, and I kicked their asses, and Hack sent them away. I don't know what he'll do with them. I can't be around the fuckers."

"I'm so sorry, Alois."

"No apologizing, beautiful." He kissed him again. "This is in no way your fault." One more kiss landed on Sebastian's mouth. "What I wanted to tell you was that, when they started talking about you, I had this moment. My dad wouldn't have hesitated to believe them when they said you were still in business."

Sebastian looked horrified. "I never wanted that, Alois. I would never choose that."

"I know," Alois said. "I know that so damn much. The thought of you willingly sleeping with someone else, for money or not, is so completely unreal to me. You love me. *Me!*"

"I do," Sebastian said.

"A gorgeous, wealthy man could walk in and tell you he loved you, but you would just shrug and say, *Sorry, but my mate is the best lover in all the galaxy. You do nothing for me.*"

Sebastian giggled. "That's what I would say?"

Alois nodded solemnly. "It is, and, in that moment

with the assholes, I realized I fully trust you, Sebastian. My head and my heart agree. They always have. I just couldn't see it. I was afraid I'd chase you off, not that you would cheat on me."

"I'm so glad," Sebastian said. "I've kind of been worried since we talked about it. My past isn't an easy thing to accept."

"Beautiful, your past didn't have a damn thing to do with my head. I never even connected your past to what my mom did until today. That was all on me. You've never given me any reason to doubt you. I just had to work through my own issues. I think they were bigger in my mind than in reality. Trusting you is so damn easy," Alois said. He pressed his forehead to Sebastian's. "Loving you is even easier. I'm sorry I've been a drama queen."

Sebastian snorted. "You haven't seen Leti when someone eats the last of his chocolate squirrels. That man is the drama queen, not you."

"I love you, Sebastian," Alois said softly. "You're my mate, but I really want you to be my husband too. How about it?"

"Nina would be yours too," Sebastian said, hiding his smile against Alois's neck.

"Uh, she already is, beautiful."

Someone cleared their throat, and Alois turned quickly. Silas and Maia sat in chairs near the window. They looked at him in sympathy and both pointed to the center of the living room floor.

Leti, Wyatt, Lilah, and Shae sat in a circle on the living room floor. Leti held Pepper in his lap. Milo was sprawled out on his back in front of him, and Sami curled into his side. Leti's wide green eyes danced with excitement and focused on Alois and Sebastian. Lilah sat gracefully next to Leti, Sophie playing in front of her. Her face was serene as usual. The woman was never anything but calm and collected, so he almost jumped when she winked at him.

On her other side, Wyatt sat cross-legged while Pela wiggled around on her belly in front of him. He gave Alois a strained smile, eyes full of sympathy. Finally, next to him sat Shae. The Siren was frozen in the process of tickling Kiki's belly, doing his best not to laugh. Nina wiggled, butt in the air, on the floor next to him. The open spot in the circle was obviously for Sebastian. Mustachio even stared at him from the perch next to the couch.

"Hi," Alois said. "I don't suppose you all went deaf for the past ten minutes or so?"

"We did not," Shae said. "I think I speak for us all when I say we're really happy you two are going to get married."

"I also speak for us all when I say that I'm not a drama queen," Leti said. "People just shouldn't eat my chocolate squirrels."

"Alois, forget them," Sebastian said, waving them away. "This is the perfect time to tell you about my dream wedding. I don't mean something like Leti's. It was perfect for him and Hack, but I don't want to get married in my backyard."

"How else could Wobble and Trixie have come?" Leti seemed baffled.

"Anything you want, beautiful," Alois said and ignored Sebastian's friends. The fuckers were moving from embarrassed silence to laughter.

Sebastian pulled away and ran up the stairs to the bedroom. "Stay right there," he yelled over his shoulder.

Alois looked around the room. "Nice day?"

"Yeah," Shae said. "It's been enlightening. Your own hasn't been so good, huh?"

"Maybe it was," Wyatt said thoughtfully. "Maybe it took meeting those jerks to make you realize you trusted Sebastian all along."

"That would make it a great day," Leti said, smiling. Princess stalked out of the kitchen, leaving a trail of crumbs behind him. Stardust was curled up, asleep, on his head. He settled next to Leti in the circle.

"Why was your dragon in my kitchen?" Alois watched Princess suspiciously.

"No reason," Leti said, vaguely. Alois stared pointedly at the trail of crumbs. Leti just smiled brightly and bounced Pepper in his lap.

Sebastian came back down the stairs before Alois could say anything else. He held up a small, bright green journal. "My family never had a lot of money for tech, so I didn't have a tablet until I bought my own when I was a teenager. It was a piece of junk, but it was mine." He handed the journal to Alois. "Anyway, my gramma gave this to me. It's my journal. Nina and I used to sit and talk about what we wanted in life, and we'd write it all down there."

"Your gramma? You never mention her," Wyatt said, tickling Pela's toes.

"She died when I was ten," Sebastian said, tears filling his eyes. "She loved me and wouldn't have let my parents sell me to clear their debt." He sniffed, then looked at the journal. "She thought Nina and I would do great things."

Alois opened the journal. "Hmm, Nina wanted to be a scientist and… create her own race of hybrid lizard people?"

"Yes," Sebastian nodded. "She was meant for greatness."

"That would have been brilliant," Leti said in awe.

Alois smiled sadly. He wished he had met Sebastian's cousin. The woman sounded like an interesting person. He turned to Sebastian's entries. "I see you wanted to be a ballet dancer. I like the twirling mustache there. You don't usually see mustachioed ballet dancers."

"Let me see!" Shae jumped up, looking over Alois's shoulder. "That's a large mustache alright." He looked at Mustachio. "I'm starting to understand your bird's name."

"Thank you," Sebastian said, nodding. "My dreams have changed, but I always wanted the mustache. They're so distinguished." He rubbed his bare upper lip and scowled. "I can't grow one though."

Alois leaned forward and kissed him. "Easier to kiss you this way." He flipped a couple of pages. "Oh, wow. That's a very detailed drawing of your dream wedding. Everyone wears elaborate, fancy hats?"

"I thought about it a lot," Sebastian said. "Granted, I was eight, but it's my dream."

"We both wear white?"

"Yes. Of course, we were both supposed to be virgins too."

"We'll pretend," Alois said, ignoring the snickers. "That's a very large cake and a… Is that a unicorn?"

"I was eight, Alois," Sebastian said, scowling when Alois started laughing.

"This will take some time, beautiful," he finally managed through his laughter.

"I know. I'm not in any hurry," Sebastian said. He grabbed Alois's hand. "I know you're mine."

10

Sebastian settled his head on Alois's shoulder. He watched the dim light from outside dance across the red scales covering his mate's chest as he slept. There were gouges from healed wounds, but Alois was a beautiful man. He was a good man too. Sebastian's heart hurt for what Alois's parents had put him through as a child.

He closed his eyes and hummed quietly, searching for Alois's threads in the spirit world. He gasped. Sebastian had seen Alois and his connection before, but it had been new and still growing. After this morning, it was a thick, unbreakable thread. Others had started growing between them too. He opened his eyes and cuddled closer to Alois, tears falling down his cheeks.

He thought of eight-year-old Sebastian, hoping with everything in him for a person to love him completely and unconditionally. That was a dream he had given up when he was seventeen and his parents sold him. Who would want a Wednesday night whore?

He thought of all the calls he received from *them*. No. They hadn't given a damn about him.

Yet, here he was, with a man who adored and loved him. A man who accepted him as he was, but still somehow believed Sebastian was the greatest thing in all the galaxy. Best of all, all of that had nothing, absolutely nothing, to do with the fact that Sebastian was his mate. He pressed his face into Alois's chest. He wouldn't let him down. He'd show Alois how much he loved him too.

SEBASTIAN, Wyatt, and Leti pushed strollers through the trade market while Maia, Silas, and Rune trailed behind them with Pax on his leash. Shae carried Sami in his arms since the little boy was a runner. It was the first day that Sebastian had managed to have off that week, and Alois and the rest of Dru's crew were busy training new recruits and keeping up with their own training routines. With the three troublemakers gone, everything was going smoothly for Alois at work, but Sebastian needed a break.

"I wonder how those three men are doing with Sheiria," Shae said.

Sebastian smiled at the man, not surprised he had known where Sebastian's thoughts had gone.

Leti smiled an evil little smile. "Will said she was determined to teach them the error of their ways."

"I can't believe they don't understand what they

did," Shae said. "A lot of things are legal on Union Station that aren't right."

Sebastian shrugged. "What's right is subjective, guys." He had accepted what had happened and moved on. There was no sense wasting time worrying about other people's morals. "Let's focus on what we're here for. Dr. Morrick said I could have today off from training, and I want to take advantage of it."

"Dr. Morrick." Wyatt mocked him. "Dad absolutely adores you, Sebastian. The least you can do is call him Verion or Death."

Sebastian blushed. "In my head, I call him Death, but I don't want to forget Dr. Morrick is in there too."

"They're both each other," Wyatt said, then shook his head. "I'm confusing myself. Okay, just call him Verion or Death. He loves you, doofus, and I know you love him too."

"I do," Sebastian agreed and nudged Wyatt in the side. "I love you too, dumb-butt."

"Aww, you two are the best," Leti said. "You love the rest of us too, right?"

"Enough of that. It's getting sticky sweet here," Shae said. "Are we looking for your wedding clothes?" Shae's eyes were stuck on a stall selling silky shirts.

"I'm going to order those from a store Ava suggested," Sebastian said. "Today, I want to find something special for Alois. Something to let him know I'm thinking of him."

"There!" Leti jumped up and down, pointing at a stall selling puppies. "Alois needs a puppy. He really, really needs a puppy."

"No," they all said at the same time.

Leti stopped bouncing and looked at them with tragic eyes. His lip quivered. "Why would you all say that?"

"Look, Leti," Shae said, wrapping his arm around Leti's shoulders. "A new pet is your answer to everything, but not everyone wants a million pets."

"Alois doesn't have a single one," Leti said. "Mustachio is Sebastian's pet, but who does Alois have? No one, that's who."

"Well, he *does* have me and Nina," Sebastian said.

Leti shook his head. "It's not the same thing." He leaned down and picked up Princess from where he lounged in the stroller between Pepper and Milo. The dragon was currently at his travel size – about a foot in length and five inches around. Leti set him on his shoulder and stroked his head, demonstrating the joys of having a pet. "Having Princess is the best."

Sebastian rolled his eyes and tuned them out. Shae and the others were still arguing with Leti, but Sebastian knew the best way to get around Leti was to ignore him. He eyed the stalls around them, all loaded down with animals. He didn't think Alois wanted a pet, but he didn't really know what kind of gift to get him. He shrugged and hummed a bit, opening his inner sight. Maybe he'd see something that called to Alois's threads.

He looked around, then found it. The threads surrounding the small animal would complement Alois's threads perfectly. He opened his eyes, then pushed Nina straight to the stall and picked up the animal. He didn't really recognize the species, though it was canine. She had thick, grey and white fur all over, but pretty light blue scales around her eyes and on her belly. On top of her head, between her floppy ears, were two little nubs for horns. Her eyes were big and blue, and her tongue hung out.

He held her up, and she licked his face. He laughed, then leaned down, letting her look at Nina. "This is Nina. Can you be nice to the baby?" The puppy nuzzled Nina's face, and his girl giggled, burying her hand in the puppy's fur.

"Hey there," the vendor said. "That's a pup from Siren's Lament. She's a month and a half old. They're really good with kids, but they get pretty big."

Sebastian knew this puppy was loving and careful. He'd seen her threads. "How much for her?" Sebastian paid the man, then awkwardly rolled Nina back over to his friends, struggling to carry the puppy too. They were still arguing, but Silas gave him a wink. The man kept an eye on everyone, not just Leti.

"All I'm saying is not everyone wants a pet as a gift, Leti," Maia said.

"They're a lot of work, and Alois has Nina to take care of," Shae said. "Kids are exhausting."

"You would know," Leti said, nodding. "Fine, we won't get him a puppy. What other ideas do we have? Sebastian, what does he like?"

They all turned to him and gaped at the puppy in his arms. "Funny story," Sebastian said. "This puppy is meant for him, so Leti was right. This time."

"Hah," Leti said, crowing. "Aww, let me see the little

girl." Sebastian handed her over, and Leti spent a few minutes petting her. "What kind of dog is she? I've never seen anything like her."

"She's from Siren's Lament," Shae said. He stopped closer so Sami could pet the puppy.

"Sebastian," Elin said, popping up right next to him.

He jumped and screeched. "Damn it, Elin."

"You all need to leave now. There's someone here that wants to hurt your friend Leti. Use your sight and you'll see it," she said, pale, shimmery face full of worry.

Sebastian closed his eyes and looked around the spirit world. At first, he didn't feel anything wrong or out of place. Then he saw it. An angry pulsing thread connected to Leti. A man stood atop a stall almost a mile away with a rifle aimed at Leti. Sebastian didn't even have to think, he followed the man's thread and channeled the fire element, burning the thread to a crisp. The man cried out and collapsed, dropping his weapon.

Sebastian opened his eyes. His friends stared at him, eyes wide. His hand was extended toward the man, smoking. "Someone was about to shoot Leti," Sebastian explained. He pointed toward the man, then realized they couldn't see him from where they were. "Come on. I'll show you."

They moved quickly, but it took a bit of time with three strollers. The man was still unconscious when they reached the stall, his body smoking. Maybe he wasn't just unconscious, Sebastian thought with a wince. No one seemed to notice him since it was so high up. The man had probably considered that when he'd chosen his location.

Silas shimmied up the poles of the stall and climbed up to the top. Sebastian watched Rune's eyes follow Silas's every move. "Like what you see?" Sebastian poked Rune in the arm.

"Yes," Rune said, sighing. "My man is so damn fine."

"I'll call it in," Maia said. "We need to figure out who he was and why he wanted Leti dead."

While they waited for enforcement to arrive, Sebastian looked to Elin. "Do you know why he wanted Leti dead?"

"No," she said. "I just felt his anger toward your friend." She stood a little taller. "Your guards were watching everything so closely, and I wanted to help so I went ahead."

"Elin says she was watching out for us too and noticed his anger toward Leti," Sebastian said. "Who have you pissed off lately?"

Leti shrugged. "The Concords, the Queen and her remaining elements, my parents' supporters and friends, and anyone Will managed to make mad."

"That's not a short list," Maia said dryly.

Silas poked his head down. "This guy is very dead, and he was a Concord. I found his communicator on him."

Sebastian felt a little sick. He'd killed a man, and it wasn't in the heat of battle like the fight with the Concords on Union Station. Wyatt wrapped an arm around him, and he leaned into his friend.

"Well, he can't have been controlled by Life," Shae said.

"We'll see what enforcement finds out," Maia said.

They arrived with Renee leading them, her face cold and merciless. "Leti, are you alright?"

"We're all fine," Leti said, hugging the woman. Sebastian hid his smile when Renee's enforcers watched in amazement as she gently smiled and hugged him back. The woman wasn't known for having the warm fuzzies.

"What happened?" Renee deftly climbed to the top as her men cleared the civilians away. Sebastian looked up and explained what happened. Silas and Maia added their own thoughts. Renee looked at Sebastian thoughtfully. "Elin told you he wanted Leti dead?"

"Basically."

"Tell her thank you," Renee said. "From all I hear, she was a good woman."

"She was," one of the enforcers said. "Haroon and Elin were friends of my wife and me." He looked at Sebastian. "You talk to her ghost? Seriously?"

Sebastian sighed. Yeah, he chose to be the weirdo instead of sticking to translating. "I do. She's a spirit for now, though she may move on eventually."

"Michael and Alvira are nice," Elin said. "You should invite them over to Leti's."

"Leti," Sebastian whispered. "Elin says you should be Michael and Alvira's friend."

"No," Elin said, amused. "I said *you* should invite them. That means you should be their friend."

"Trust me," Sebastian told her. "Leti is much better at that friend stuff than me."

"Which means you need more friends," she said.

"You aren't my dead wife, Elin, so you can't boss me around." Sebastian put his hands on his hips and stared her down.

She just smiled smugly. "Look around you, Sebastian." He looked around. Everyone was staring at him, faces full of amusement and horror both. "I'm dead, so I'll always win." She laughed and disappeared.

"Damn it!" Sebastian turned to Michael and groaned. "Elin says you and Alvira should come to Sunday dinner at Leti and Hack's house."

"Okay?" The man blinked and shrugged. "Alvira would love that, and Hack isn't horrible."

"Aww, you know my husband so well," Leti said, laughing.

"Maia, Silas," Renee said. "Get these guys home. I'll let you all know what we find out."

They left and headed home. Hack and Alois were waiting on them, both looking pissed off. "Leti, you can't leave the house again," Hack said.

"Yeah, that's not going to work," Leti said. He pushed the stroller to Hack, then took Sami from Shae. The Siren took one look at Hack and laughed. He pushed past them into the house. Leti sighed. "Will, we have a lot of enemies, but I also have a lot of friends. Sebastian saved the day, and Maia and Silas are always with me."

"The Concords want you dead," Hack said. "Until they're dealt with, you need to be cautious."

"Yes," Leti said, nodding. "However, cautious doesn't mean staying locked in the house forever."

"I'm increasing your guards," Hack said, running his hands through his hair. "Silas and Maia are only two people, and the Concords have too damn many."

"That's not a bad idea," Silas said. "We could send someone ahead and have someone following behind every time we go out."

They all went into Leti's house and unloaded the babies. "I wonder why they specifically want Leti dead," Wyatt said. "He's still researching the Queen, but Dad and I are the ones that are trying to permanently kill them."

"Are you jealous?" Leti wiggled his eyebrows, and Wyatt laughed.

"It's no secret that Fasi declared this war at Leti's behest," Alois said. "The Concords have lost a lot, and Admiral Sharp is probably pissed. Leti is the public face of this war."

Leti set Sami down and headed for the kitchen. "I'm heating up one of Ma's casseroles. If we have to talk about this shit, then I'm eating lunch."

"Already ahead of you," Shae said. "It's in the oven."

Sebastian watched Alois roll his shoulders and rub his eyes. His poor mate was worried for them all. He took the puppy from Maia and nibbled his lip. After a moment, he held her out to Alois. "I got you a present."

Alois stared at the puppy. "Huh?"

"I love you like Leti loves his chocolate squirrels," Sebastian said. "I wanted to get you something special to show you how much I appreciate you. She's perfect for you, Alois. I know she is."

Alois's brown eyes softened, and he smiled. "Thank you, beautiful," he said and took the puppy. Alois held her away from his body, and the puppy just panted happily and stared at him in adoration. "I, uh, love it."

"You will," Sebastian said, laughing at the perplexed look on Alois's face. His mate might not realize it, but Sebastian had just given him the perfect companion. The threads didn't lie.

$\mathcal{A}$lois dressed Nina in his favorite outfit. He slipped the black leggings on her, then pulled the miniature, black and blue uniform shirt over her head. He tickled her belly, then tugged on her blue tutu and put her little black boots on her feet. "There's my little Blue Solace girl," Alois said. He picked her up and pressed kisses to her face. Nina giggled and shook her head. Her fine, black hair slid into her eyes, and he brushed it back.

"Are you already starting her training?" Cordelia was curled on the window seat between Alois's pride and joy, Periwinkle, and Ava.

"She's going to be the best little Blue Solace girl ever," Alois said and kissed her chubby cheeks again. He turned his attention to Cordy. She played with Peri's ears and rubbed his dog's little horns. Peri had grown into a huge, long-limbed puppy in three months. He was getting the idea that she would be massive when fully grown.

"Did Dru tell you about Icewilde?" Ava kissed the top of Peri's head. The prime diplomat of Blue Sector always looked put together. Ava was a fighter, but she loved the latest fashions and relished her new duties. They gave her more time to wear fancy clothes.

Alois winced. "Yeah. That's the third planet Air has ravaged." It also wasn't a vacation spot like the other two. Millions more died on Icewilde than either Bredell or Dairilve. "Beol and his team are on Air's trail, but the fucker seems to always be a step ahead of him."

"Do you remember when we first met Dr. Morrick?" Ava looked thoughtful. "He said his supervisors were working with someone, and if the artifact fell into their hands, billions would die."

"Billions *have* died," Alois said. "It just didn't involve Death's artifact."

"It just seems so strange that Admiral Sharp and the Queen would fall in together so quickly after she was resurrected," Ava said. She shook her head. "I don't know. Something is there, but I can't find it."

Cordelia frowned and stared at her lap.

"What's going on, Cordelia?" Alois asked.

Ava frowned at their friend, just then noticing Cordelia's unusual silence.

"It seems stupid to think about when there's so much shit to work on with the Queen and the Concords," Cordelia said.

"Anything that upsets you is important, sweet pea," Ava said.

"I'm in love with Quinn," she said, tears filling her

eyes. "I was so set on just being her friend so I wouldn't lose her. Now she has a date with fucking Liam Doney."

"The pilot?" Ava's eyes widened, and Alois didn't blame her. The man was damn good-looking. Not as handsome as Sebastian, but still a catch.

"Yes," Cordelia said, hissing.

"Hmm," Alois said. He sat in the window seat beside Peri. His girl laid her head on his shoulder and panted happily. "She hasn't dated anyone since you guys talked months ago?"

"No," Cordelia said and peeled at the polish on her fingernails. "We've been spending our free time together, hanging out."

"Now, you want to date her." Ava grinned.

"Yes," Cordelia said, teeth clenched.

"Then tell her," Alois said, shrugging. "Cordelia, she adores you."

"It's been over five months since I told her we needed to stay friends," Cordelia said.

"Things change. You wanted her then, and you want her now. Are you willing to let Liam Doney walk away with her?" Alois gave her a look.

"Fuck him," Cordelia growled.

"That's my girl," Alois said, patting her on the back. "Go to Quinn right now and tell her how you feel. If she doesn't want you anymore, then okay. You tried. You have to try, Cordy. You'll regret it if you don't."

"You're right," she said, standing. "Alright. I'm doing it." She started toward the door, then turned back. "If she turns me down, do you guys want to eat junk food and watch Love's Perfect Match?"

"Definitely," Alois said. "Nina loves that show." Nina chewed on her fist and ignored him.

"I'm sure she does," Ava said, standing. "Come on. I'll help you pick out an outfit."

Cordelia groaned and the two left. Alois stood and found Nina's baby sling. He strapped it on and stuck her in it, then headed downstairs with Peri. Sebastian stood at the kitchen window, looking out into Leti's backyard.

"Are Rune and Silas snuggling again?"

"Nope," Sebastian said. "Mo and Alex are having a pet battle in the backyard. Damn, Fluffle is fierce."

"She's Selene's cat," Alois said. "Of course, she's fierce." He watched the small, fluffy cat jump over Princess Buttercup and smack Gravy in the nose. The big dog yelped and lay down, paws over his nose. "Fierce," he said, awed. He shook his head. "You ready to go?"

"Yes," Sebastian said, then opened the window, so Mustachio could go outside if he wanted. "I'm starving to death."

"To death?"

"Can't you tell?" Sebastian looked at him with big eyes and pouty lips.

"You're wasting away," Alois said, nodding gravely. "Let's go feed you." He grabbed Peri's leash, then they left the house, holding hands, and headed toward Juniper's.

The diner was busy when they got there, but they

found seats near the window at a table with Wyatt and his family. Sebastian hustled forward, hugging Wyatt. "I haven't seen you in a week, Wyatt. What gives?"

"Dad and I are working on the artifacts," Wyatt said, yawning. "We're close."

"Alois," Remy said, coming to take their order. "You better put Peri in the backyard before Juniper sees you. No pets except dragons and newts allowed in the restaurant."

"Fine," Alois said, scowling. He gave Remy his order, then walked Peri out the back door to a fenced-in area. Porkchop ran around the yard with Biscuit. They stopped when they saw him come out and came over to sniff Peri. Peri barked, then the three ran off to play. "Silly animals."

He turned around and ran into Juniper. The man had his comm out, and Alois recognized the new manager of the gardens for the Blue Sector. "I don't know what's wrong with the corn," the man said. "Can't you come take a look?"

"I have a restaurant to run," Juniper said, then sighed. "I'll come out when my shift ends." He ended the call, then collapsed against Alois, his head landing on Alois's shoulder. "Why is life so hard?"

"You need to take a break, Juniper," Alois said. The poor man had bags under his eyes. "Is the new guy bothering you too much?"

"Every single day," Juniper said. They walked back to the table. "He knows his stuff but has zero experience."

"Do you know what's wrong?"

"I think so, but I'll need to see it." Juniper plopped into the chair next to Morgan. He held his arms out. "Give me a baby."

Morgan handed him Pela. "There you go."

Alois grinned as his friend started cooing, stress melting away. He took Sebastian's hand and sipped his drink. His mate was talking quietly with Death. "I've taught you everything I can," Death said. "I wish I was more helpful, but everything else I know is half-remembered."

"I can't believe all I *have* learned," Sebastian said. "Leti and I are searching for more guides. Thank you, Dr. Morrick. I really think we can save Fire."

"Me too," Death said. "If he ever gets here."

"It has been a while," Wyatt said. "I hate having this attack hanging over our shoulders."

"The whole station is on edge," Juniper said. "Grellweir and Fallow already sent some ships to add to our fleet. Cardinal Hold, Haven, and Siren's Lament are patrolling the system." He smiled. "I can't believe how much our system has pulled together. We've always had good relationships but not like this."

"I think it's Fasi and the council," Alois said. "Fasi is well liked and the council has connections to each planet. Together, they're a hell of a team."

"They are," Juniper agreed. His comm chimed again and he groaned. "Fucking corn."

"What's wrong?" Sebastian asked. "That sounds like a Leti curse."

"The new manager for the gardens in Blue Sector keeps bugging Juny about the corn," Alois said. He stretched his arm around Sebastian's seat and smiled when his mate leaned into him.

"Hmm," Sebastian said and closed his eyes. Alois watched him carefully, knowing he was looking through the spirit world. His friends kept talking around him but quieted when a soft, green light surrounded Sebastian.

"What is he doing?" Alois looked to Morrick.

"I think he's looking at the gardens," Death said, eyeing Sebastian. "I can feel him using the life element."

The glow around Sebastian grew brighter when Mustachio flew by the window and landed on the fence. Hector crowed, establishing his dominance, and Miss Speckles eyed Mustachio suspiciously before returning to people watching.

Sebastian's eyes popped open and he grinned. "I think I've fixed what was wrong with the corn. The threads were all goopy."

"Is that your professional opinion?" Juniper said. "They were goopy?"

Sebastian rolled his eyes and stuck out his tongue.

"Children, really," Remy said, delivering their food.

Juniper's comm chimed, and he answered it. A young Grell popped up, wringing his hands. "Holy shit, Juniper. You'll never believe what just happened."

"Tell me, Astus," Juniper said. He shot a look to Sebastian. Alois's mate smiled serenely.

"Right after we talked, this green light just appeared around all the crops. It just stayed there a second, then it disappeared," Astus said. "The corn is just fine now. All the other crops look ten times better too."

"Well," Juniper said and tossed a biscuit at Sebastian. "To think a few minutes of our local shaman's time has saved you and me a shit load of worry."

"Shaman? That's real?" Astus asked. "I heard rumors about a guy, but I thought that was bullshit."

Juniper turned his comm around. "Meet Sebastian the Phenomenal, Charybdis Station's only shaman."

Sebastian looked thoughtful as he bit into the biscuit Juniper had thrown at him. "'The Phenomenal,' huh? I like it."

"Thank you," Astus said, stuttering.

"No problem," Sebastian said. "I'll check in on the crops once a week and see if they need a boost. You guys are doing really well. The plants are happy."

"Happy?" The young man looked horrified. "We're going to eat them."

"Everything has a cycle, Astus," Juniper said, grinning. "Bye, buddy." He closed the comm. "That was interesting."

Alois hugged his mate. "Good work, beautiful."

Sebastian grinned. "I helped Charybdis Station."

"Yes, you did," Wyatt said, eyes soft as he watched Sebastian. "We told you that you were wonderful."

"I'm phenomenal," Sebastian corrected. "Sebastian the Phenomenal."

Alois started laughing and couldn't stop. "Oh fuck. At least that's better than Yusuf the Terrible."

Juniper and Morgan started laughing too. "Leti and he *are* best friends, Alois. You had to know this was coming," Morgan said.

Morgan, Wyatt, and Death just watched Alois and his friends laugh.

Sebastian sniffed. "Ignore them. They can't handle the fact that Leti and I have well-known, fantastic names and they don't." He typed out a message to Leti, then worked on finishing his breakfast.

"You are too cute," Juniper said, wiping his eyes. "Okay, back to work. Enjoy breakfast, guys." He left them to it, and they polished off their plates.

ALOIS AND SEBASTIAN held hands as they walked toward the tram with Hack. They had just finished dropping Nina and Peri off with Shae and were headed to the weekly strategy meeting. Fire's fleet may have been moving slowly, but they were on the way, and Fasi believed in being as prepared as possible.

"Now, Leti thinks he needs to go with us to meet Fire," Hack grumbled. "He said Yusuf and Sebastian can't be parted."

Alois laughed. "You know we're not letting him go, right?" He eyed Hack. "You know that you're not going either, right? Hack, right?" Hack avoided his eyes. "You need to stay to lead the fleet in case it doesn't work."

Hack huffed. "Fine. It's just that Selene insists on going, and I always fight beside her. It's just weird not to go."

"Dru will take care of things," Alois said. "Morgan and I will be there too."

"It still doesn't feel right," Hack said. "Anyway, has Cordelia called yet?"

Alois grinned. "Nope. I heard Liam Doney was seen having dinner with his friends instead of out with a date." Hack and Alois shared amused looks.

They entered Fasi's favorite conference room together and found seats. Sheiria was already there. Cas and Audre were on vid-screens, and the other five people planning on accompanying Death to meet Fire spread out around the table. It was decided to keep the group small, so the Concords might actually buy the whole diplomatic ploy. It would just be Death, Sebastian, Alois, Dru, Morgan, and Selene. Alois hoped that would be enough to protect Sebastian. It didn't hurt that one of Beol's assassins was still on board too. Hopefully.

Haroon dropped into the seat next to Sebastian.

"Haroon, what are you doing here?" Sebastian leaned across Alois to frown at his friend.

"I talked with the Lord Admiral, and he said I could go too," Haroon said. He sent Sebastian a small smile. "You're my friend now, Sebastian, and I've got your back. My sole purpose will be guarding you while the others do their thing. My lieutenant is stepping up to captain my ship during the battle."

"You'd better not do anything crazy," Morgan said, eyes narrowed. "I know you lost Elin not too long ago, but no one dies on this mission. Got it?"

Haroon saluted. "Yes, sir."

Alois smiled half-heartedly but couldn't help but remember Pela and Kiki. He didn't blame Morgan for being suspicious. Their friends had sure as shit saved the day, but they'd died doing it. Fasi came into the room looking grim, followed by a cold-faced Renee. Something big had happened.

"Alright, everyone," Fasi said. "Fire and his fleet will enter the system in two days."

"So soon?" Sebastian's hands fidgeted.

"Yes," Fasi said, sending him a sympathetic look. "Cas, Audre, and the Half-Moon Assassins slowed them down and picked off a number of their ships. Mysterious engine malfunctions also ruined quite a few. They lost about a third of their fleet on the way here."

"That's still too many ships left," Hack said.

"It is," Renee said. "Our best hope is that Death and Sebastian are able to free Fire. Otherwise, we don't stand much of a chance against them."

"We'll fight," Sheiria said. "No matter what."

"We'll be there too," Cas said. "Audre's coming into the system near Siren's Lament, and I'll be coming in near Grellweir."

Fasi looked at each one of them. "Charybdis Station will fight to the death if need be. Grellweir and Fallow have agreed to have ships ready to evacuate the station if it comes to it."

"It won't," Sebastian said, voice strong and steady. "I *will* free Fire, and Death *will* take out the Concord fleet. Believe it and plan accordingly." He looked around the room at the shocked faces. "Let's talk about how we're going to get on that flagship."

Sebastian the Phenomenal, Alois thought.

Two days later, Sebastian stood with Leti and his two shadows at the docks watching Dru and Lerais kiss each other goodbye. "Do you think they'll ever stop?" Sebastian really thought they would have had to come up for air by now.

Leti tilted his head and stared at them. "At least they're just kissing."

The place was bustling since Fire's fleet entered the system an hour ago. Sebastian and Alois had said goodbye to Nina and left her, Peri, and Mustachio with Shae at the daycare. The Siren's job was to make sure Blue Sector's kids and pets survived. Shae and his workers would get them to a ship if they needed to evacuate. Leti and his guards would be with them, guarding them with their lives.

Sebastian was so damn nervous. If he failed, the station would be destroyed, and his friends would probably die. Nina would probably die.

"Sebastian," Leti said, turning around and grabbing

his hand. It was weird to see Leti without one of the kids. He looked half-dressed. His friend smiled at him, green eyes sparkling. "You can do this. I know it."

"I have to," Sebastian said. "There's no other option."

Leti leaned in and hugged him. "Princess Buttercup wants to go with you."

Sebastian felt Princess crawl to his shoulder. "Leti, I can't take Princess."

"It's not your choice," Leti said. "It's not my choice. It's Princess's choice."

Princess shrunk on his shoulder until he was only six inches long and about half an inch around. He crawled down Sebastian's neck, under his shirt, and onto his back. Sebastian shuddered. "Eww, that's so creepy."

"He's well-known now," Leti said. "He'll hide until the fight. Make sure you give him a couple of shields, alright?" He handed Sebastian a handful of shield buttons.

"I'll take care of him," Sebastian said and hugged his friend again. "I know how much you love him."

Leti sniffled. "I love you too, Sebastian. Besides, he's a Charybdis soldier and wants to protect our home and family."

Alois and Morgan jogged up. "It's time, beautiful. Fasi just finished speaking with Admiral Sharp. They think we're returning Death and sending a diplomatic group to talk."

"Leti, will you take Stardust?" Morgan kissed the baby dragon and handed him to Leti. "I can't find Princess, and someone needs to keep an eye on my boy.

Wyatt and Luna are already on one of the medical ships."

"Of course," Leti said and put the dragon on his shoulder. "You all be careful, alright? When this is over, we're having a big meal at my house, and I'm hugging each and every one of you." He nodded sharply, then turned and headed toward Hack.

"I love him so much," Sebastian said. "I love them all – Wyatt, Shae, and all the others."

Alois cuddled him close. "I know, beautiful. We'll do our best to keep everyone safe, so we can see them again." They walked into the shuttle and sat. Everyone strapped in, and Sebastian did his best not to squash Princess.

Fasi stood at the door. "I'm so damn proud of each and every one of you," he said. "Charybdis was blessed the day each of you came to us, and there is no one I trust more with this mission." He looked over Alois, Morgan, and the others before focusing on the two civilians. "Dr. Morrick, thank you for taking this chance. I know you don't want to go back to her, and this is a risk for you. Sebastian, I love you, son. You had best come back, understand?"

"Yes, sir," Sebastian said, nodding. That was definitely Plan A. Mustachio flew into the shuttle door, startling Fasi. The Lord Admiral yelped and spun around when the bird soared over his head. "Mustachio, no." The bird ignored him and settled on the back of Alois's seat.

"He's here for a reason, Sebastian," Death said.

"Remember, it's his tail feathers decorating your stomach."

"Fine," Sebastian said. "You better not get hurt, sweetheart."

"Don't worry, beautiful," Alois said. "I'll be fine." Mustachio started pecking through Alois's hair. "Stupid bird." Sebastian giggled.

"Good luck, guys," Fasi said and saluted them. He left and the door closed. The shuttle took off, and Sebastian swallowed hard. Looking out the window, he noticed they passed ship after ship. The fleet was headed toward the battle.

"Alright," Dru said. "Remember, Death freezes and distracts Fire. Sebastian works on the binding, and we watch their backs." Monty perched on her shoulder and looked ready for battle. *Well, as much as a newt can be ready*, Sebastian thought.

"Admiral Sharp is likely to be there," Selene said, voice flat and face blank. "I have some presents for him."

Dru grinned. "Me too. Damn, but I love this blade of Beol's."

"Beck gave us some goodies too," Morgan said, pulling out a bag. He passed it around, and everyone took out a small, mechanical ball. "These little buggers should only be used in a group of bad guys though. He said to stay at least ten feet away from them when they go off."

"Sebastian," Elin said, appearing in front of him.

Sebastian jumped and squeaked. "Damn it, Elin."

"I checked over there and the Concord leader just

told his men to kill everyone but Death when you arrive. He doesn't care that you're supposed to be diplomats."

"Fuck," Sebastian said. "Guys, Elin did some recon, and she says they plan on killing us as soon as we're off the shuttle."

"No pretense then," Selene said. "We go in fighting."

"I will harvest everyone I can and go straight to Fire," Death said. "I don't know how many I can get before he requires my full attention."

"We all follow Death to the bridge," Dru said. "From there, we can hold off the Concords until Death and Sebastian do their thing. We need to stay together."

"I'll go scout ahead," Elin said. "I'll let you know if I find anything."

Sebastian brought his and Alois's linked hands up to kiss his mate's knuckles. "I have a secret weapon riding on my back."

"Huh?" Alois said.

"Princess decided he wanted to come," Sebastian said.

"That improves our odds. If we had known our cover wouldn't matter, we could have stuffed the shuttle with soldiers," Dru said. "We'll make it fast and get to the bridge as soon as we can." Princess Buttercup crawled over his shoulder and hissed. Dru rolled her eyes. "I'm sure there will be plenty of Concords to kill along the way, Princess. Fuck, now *I'm* talking to him."

"Approaching the flagship," Morgan said from the pilot's seat. "Look at that." The man sounded pleased, so they looked out the windows. Charybdis' generals were ready. The Blue and Yellow fleets lay front and center, ready to take on the Concords. Unfortunately, they looked tiny in comparison to the Concords' masses. "To the left, guys. Look to the left."

"That's Cas," Dru said. "Along with a fucking fleet of Grell."

"General Shepard is coming up on the other side with the Yellow fleet and a bunch of Siren ships," Haroon said.

"There's the Fallon and the Cardinals," Alois said, grinning as the two fleets came to a stop behind Sheiria and Hack's ships. Sebastian didn't blame him. Their numbers were starting to even out. "How much do you want to bet the Havenites are filling up our medical ships?"

"Who are those ships?" Sebastian pointed to another large fleet coming to join Hack and Sheiria's ships. The newcomers were a mishmash of colors and ship types.

"Fuck me," Morgan said. "That's three different mercenary groups. I knew they had allied with us, but this is… This is fucking great."

Dru grinned and pulled out her phaser and blade. "Everyone activate your shields. We have a job to do."

"Come on, Princess," Sebastian said. "No sense in hiding." The dragon crawled to his shoulder, and Sebastian attached a shield to his back, activating it. "I'll add more when you get bigger."

They landed and everyone stood, pulling out their weapons. Death stood in front of the door and closed his eyes. Grey wisps poured through the walls of the ship, pulled straight to him, and he absorbed them all. The man's eyes popped open when the inner wires within the shuttle door exploded. The door slid off, landing with a hard thump.

"Well, Fire knows we're here," Death said. "Move fast." He darted out the door, and they followed him. They ran through the halls of the massive ship, and Death led them, mind already focused on Fire. "I have him frozen, but I must focus on him."

"Selene," Dru said. "With me." The two women took lead. Mustachio soared above them, easily keeping pace.

Dru darted to the front, phasers pulled. She easily shot and killed the few Concords they came across. "There's not many of them here," she said suspiciously.

A woman materialized in front of them, hands raised. "I'm with Half-Moon." They lowered their weapons. "You all need some help?"

"Wondered if you were still on board," Dru said. "We're headed to the bridge. Name?"

"Clara," she said.

"Welcome to the fight, Clara," Dru said, and then they were moving again, Clara falling in line with them.

Elin was suddenly running beside him. "There's a group ahead. They're waiting to ambush you."

"Elin says there's an ambush ahead."

"Around the next two corners."

Sebastian repeated her words, and Dru laughed. "I love you, Elin!"

"Hey," Haroon said. "That's my dead wife you're talking to."

"What?" Clara looked at them in confusion.

"The joys of a shaman's life." Alois tugged Sebastian to the side and shot a Concord soldier. The man had been hiding under one of the collapsed bodies in the hall.

They approached the corner, and Selene pulled two of Beck's new toys from her pack. She activated them and tossed them, allowing the devices to bounce against the wall and land around the corner. Less than a second later, they heard screams of pain. They walked around the corner. Sebastian held his hand to his mouth. The Concords had been electrocuted by whatever Beck had created. The bodies shook and some still sizzled with blue lightning.

"Damn, Beck does like electricity," Dru said. "Come on. Keep moving."

"We're almost there," Elin said. "Before the bridge, there are two rooms, one on each side of the hall. Right now, the doors are shut, but there are groups waiting in each room for you to pass by. They plan to pin you against the bridge door."

"Damn it," Sebastian said. "Thank you, Elin." He told the others what she had found.

"Hmm," Dru said. "This might be harder than we thought."

"Princess and I have the room to the right," Sebastian said. "You all can take the other."

"What? I don't think so, beautiful."

"Okay. Princess, *Alois*, and I have the room to the

right. You all have the other." Sebastian was starting to flag. He really needed to start jogging every morning.

"How do we get in and maintain the surprise?" Dru wasn't even panting. *Bitch!*

"Here it is," Elin said, popping in front of the group. They stopped before reaching the doors.

"Like this," Sebastian said. He closed his eyes, entering the spirit world, and focused on the circuits running through the walls. He pulled their threads and held his hands out. To each side of him, the walls imploded, and the ship rocked. His eyes opened. He may have gone through more than one wall. *Oops!*

"Fuck, Sebastian," Dru said and shook her head.

"How did you do that?" Clara watched him with wide eyes.

"No time for explanations. Move it, guys," Dru said.

Princess jumped from his shoulder and grew, roaring loudly as he entered the room. Sebastian quickly slapped more shields on him and activated them, so his large size was covered. The dragon was easily fifteen feet long and five feet wide by the time he finished expanding. The large group of Concords didn't fare well. The dragon breathed a large wave of fire, covering most of the room. Alois fired into the mess, picking off the few mercenaries that managed to survive.

"Well, that went fast," Alois said, looking around at the destruction. "Come on, guys. Let's help the others." Sebastian could hear them from where he stood.

Princess shrank to fit through the hole, then joined the battle in the second room. Alois hopped in behind him, phasers firing. Sebastian was about to follow, but Death stood in the hallway, eyes focused on the bridge door.

"I can't hold him any longer," Death said. "Sebastian, we need to do this. Their fleet is already attacking ours."

If Fire was free, he could hurt their fleet, giving the Concords a huge advantage.

"Princess," he yelled, then held his hand out, focusing on the door. It blew inside, and Death ran through it. "Fuck, fuck, fuck."

He looked back toward the others, but they were busy. Princess slipped out, hissing as he came to a stop beside Sebastian. A small line of blood trickled down Princess's side. He put more shields on the dragon and activated them.

"Ready to do this?"

The dragon entered the bridge with a roar, and Sebastian followed behind him. He ducked behind a small console and looked for Fire. Princess was holding his own against the Concords, but there were a lot of them. Sebastian couldn't see through all the chaos. He closed his eyes and searched the spirit world. As he looked for Fire, he cut the threads of as many Concords as he could. He didn't want to kill them, but he shook his head and thought of the fleets fighting outside.

"Damn it, Sebastian." Haroon's voice startled him.

Sebastian opened his eyes and saw Haroon standing over him, fighting off Concords. Alois stood with him, face grim. Sebastian closed his eyes again and focused, knowing he was safe. A bright mess of beautiful, pure threads drew his attention. The sweet, fiery threads were corralled by sickly green ones. The binding. He opened his eyes and poked his head above the console. He ignored the dead bodies and fighting and focused on the slim collar around an old man's neck.

The man was human like the rest, but he was a lot older than the others, with grey hair and a wrinkled and weathered face. His eyes gave him away. They swirled with fire, looking remarkably like Hack's when he was drawing his fire to him. The man's expression was empty as he focused on Death. He threw something toward Sebastian's friend. They were small, sticky patches, and he'd never seen anything like them. Death froze them in the air, letting them drop far away from him. Occasionally, one got through, and Death dodged to the side. It all looked ridiculous. Sebastian expected some fierce, showy battle.

Sebastian took a second to look at the patches and blanched. Bindings. If any of those even touched Death, he was the Queen's. "Fuck. Alois, Haroon, we need to stop him now or we'll lose Death. Princess," he yelled, jumping up and running through the room. The dragon roared and followed, swiping and biting men as he went. Alois followed on Sebastian's heels, shooting anyone in their way, and Haroon cursed and followed, shooting his phaser as he ran.

Sebastian focused on Fire's binding and began the process of unraveling it. It was hard to do while he ran. He couldn't focus enough. As if he had summoned him, Mustachio's song filled the air, a deep hum that was as familiar to Sebastian as Alois's voice. He easily slipped into the spirit world, his body still moving. The binding was all he could see and within a few moments, he'd unraveled the Queen's work. It was built with such ugliness. Hate, envy, and cruelty. She enjoyed knowing how much she hurt Fire.

The binding fell to the ground and Fire froze, dropping the binding patches. He looked at Sebastian and blinked. Death stopped moving and looked around the room. The fighting was slowing down, so the element quickly went to the wide window and watched the ships fighting. Sebastian looked around too. There weren't many alive in the room anymore. Dru and the others had joined them and were finishing off the Concords. He counted people, breathing a sigh of relief that everyone was alive. Mustachio landed next to him and leaned his head against Sebastian's leg. He stroked his bird's head, so glad he had come to help.

Alois pulled him into his arms, chin settling on his head, and they watched the last of the mercenaries fall. One Concord man stood out from the others. He was middle-aged and dressed in the finest clothes Sebastian had ever seen. His face was screwed up with hate, and he ran toward Fire, binding patch in his hand.

"Princess," Sebastian yelled and pointed. Princess pounced, launching across the room and landing on the man. Sebastian winced as the man's body was squashed. That was just gross. The dragon leaned down and bit the dead man's head off, spitting it toward the door.

"Princess," Selene said, blades falling to her sides. "I

wanted to kill Admiral Sharp." The dragon rumbled and rubbed his head against Selene. "Of course, I forgive you."

"He's so pretty! Can I pet him?" Fire bounced in place beside Princess. "Please? Please? Please?" Sebastian and his friends stared at the ancient being. "Who's a pretty boy? Who?" Fire scratched Princess's nose, and the dragon rumbled happily.

"What. The. Fuck!" Dru exclaimed.

*A*lois held Sebastian and finally took a breath. Damn, but he didn't like his mate being in battle. He had some crazy skills, but one of them *wasn't* basic observation. Alois had stopped counting the number of times Sebastian had almost been shot or stabbed without noticing it.

Dru finished off the last merc and turned to them. "Death, can you help our guys?"

"It will take time and effort, but I will," Death said. "I'll start by freezing the ships. There are a lot of them though, so I'll have to wait to deal with the Concords."

"I can help," Fire said. He gave Princess a kiss on the nose, then went to stand close to Death. He scrunched up his nose. "I won't kill them, but I can make their engines and weapon systems malfunction."

"That would help, Fire. Thank you," Death said.

"I want to help you," Fire said, voice small. "I tried to hurt you in our last cycle. You were beautiful and in love, but the Queen made me try to hurt you."

Death wrapped an arm around the old man. "I understand. I understood then too." He closed his eyes, and Fire did the same. "Let's save these people. You'll like them, Fire. I know you will."

Over the next five minutes, each ship in the Concord fleet lost their engines and then their weapons. The fighting came to a standstill, and then Death began his work. The grey, delicate souls poured from the Concord ships to Death. Alois could imagine what the ships looked like, soulless, collapsed bodies lying everywhere. He shivered. He had to admit he was glad he wouldn't have to board the ships to check for the Concord's prisoners.

"Fuck," Clara said, standing next to Alois and Sebastian. "What are those?"

"Souls," Sebastian said. "He can harvest the souls of people, leaving them alive, but empty. From what we've seen, the bodies just lay there, breathing."

Clara looked horrified. "Yeah. It's not pleasant," Alois said. "It saves our soldiers' lives though."

"I can get with that," she said, shaking her head. "We've seen some crazy shit in the Crellic System, but this makes me really glad he's on our side." She looked toward Fire. "He was seriously creepy with that collar on. He just stared blankly and did exactly what Sharp told him to do."

"Not anymore," Sebastian said firmly. "We'll keep him away from the Queen and her bindings." Alois kissed the top of his head. He had the feeling they would have a guest staying with them for a while.

Fire came to them, leaving Death to his harvest.

"You freed me," he said, eyes big and full of tears. He launched himself at them, and Alois found himself hugging two men. Sebastian sniffled, then both men started crying. Alois sighed. They would definitely have a houseguest for the foreseeable future.

"I called Hack and asked for a pick-up," Dru said. "We still need to clean out the ship. No one has come to attack, but that doesn't mean they aren't hiding out somewhere."

"Oh," Fire said, wiping his eyes. "The admiral kept some people in cages near his quarters."

"I can show you where they are," Clara said.

"Okay," Dru said. "Alois, will you and Clara go find the prisoners? Selene, Morgan, Princess, and I will start clearing the ship."

"Got it," Alois said, reluctantly releasing Sebastian. "I'll see you soon, beautiful. Stay here with Haroon and Death." He looked at Fire. "Will you make sure he stays safe?"

Fire nodded furiously. "Yes, yes, yes. I'll protect him so good." Mustachio flew to the back of a chair, and Fire's eyes followed him. "Oh, look at him. He's so distinguished." He started stroking Mustachio's feathered head.

Sebastian laughed and took his hand. "Just like a mustache, right? My name is Sebastian. Come on. Let's sit down and talk while they do what they do best." They headed to some chairs close to Death, and Haroon followed behind. Sebastian looked over his shoulder. "Elin says there are three groups of Concords left on the ship. One really small group near the prisoners, and two larger ones in the ship's commons and training rooms."

"At least they're not all over the place," Dru said, moaning as she pulled her blade out again. "Damn, but I'm tired." She had a gash on her head and a shot to her shoulder, but she was still fighting.

"Remember to keep Princess shielded," Sebastian said, settling into a chair and yawning.

"We will," Dru said, patting Princess's flank. "This guy is my hero." Princess hissed, and she moved her hand. "He's still a jerk though."

Alois and Clara left the bridge, running toward the admiral's quarters. "Why did he keep them so close to his quarters?"

Clara didn't answer at first, then huffed. "He used them. Every single fucking night." She wouldn't meet his eyes. "I didn't do anything for them. I couldn't blow my cover, and they suffered, Alois. A lot."

"Fuck, Clara," Alois said. "I don't know what to say. You did what you had to do, but that sucks."

"Yeah," she said. "I'm used to it in a way. Before Beol took over, our Guild Master made us do some sick shit. We didn't have much choice in it either since he would hurt our families or friends if we didn't obey." She took a deep breath when they reached a closed door. "I'm not used to saving people."

"You've already saved so many, Clara. The intel you provided helped us pull this off. Now, let's take care of these people."

Alois raised his guns, and Clara went low, pushing open the door and rolling into the room. The six mercenaries were ready for an attack, but they still went down fast. Clara's blades moved fast as she cut down two before they could react. Alois fired his phasers, focusing on one merc's head until the man's shield gave. Alois pulled his vibro-blade and finished off another when the woman rushed him. By then, Clara was on the last one, and Alois looked around the room.

Seven cages lined the back wall, each holding three people. At least they were adults, though barely. They were a mix of species, both men and women. Each was clean and dressed in filmy night clothes, and each wore a look of hope as they watched the last mercenary fall to the floor.

"Hi," Alois said. "We're from Charybdis Station and are here to rescue you. Give us a second, and we'll get these cages open."

Clara raised her hand in the air. "Keycard!"

"Good eyes," Alois said, and they quickly opened the cages. He looked around, but there were no personal belongings, little less shoes. "I'm sorry we don't have anything else for you to wear right now, but we'll get you folks set up when we get back to the station."

"We're really free?" The woman was tiny. Her large grey eyes were fragile, and she looked like she didn't quite believe them.

"You are," Clara said. "Come on. Let's get the hell out of here." They led them slowly back to the bridge. Death still stood at the window, but the flow of souls had stopped. Fire stood with him, arms wrapped around Death's waist, head leaning on his shoulder.

Sebastian jumped out of his seat and ran to the group.

"Are any of you injured? We have medical supplies back on our shuttle," Sebastian said. He pulled off his black and blue uniform coat and wrapped it around one of the smaller, shivering rescued prisoners.

"We're alright," a young man said, voice bitter. "They kept us healthy and well fed."

"There's more than one way to hurt," Sebastian said, eyes sad. Alois pulled him into his arms again. Fuck, but he hated that his Sebastian knew that so well. Sebastian leaned his head against Alois chest, right over his heart.

"I love you, beautiful," Alois whispered.

"I love you too, Alois," Sebastian said. "You and Haroon did a damn good job keeping me safe. I'm sorry I'm so inexperienced."

"I'm not. I'd rather you never have to go into battle."

"You two are mates?" the gray-eyed woman asked.

"We are," Sebastian said. "We also happen to love each other." The woman's smile lit up her face.

Dru and the others came back. The freed prisoners ran to hide behind Alois and Sebastian when Princess came stomping in.

"Ship's cleared," Dru said and dropped into one of the seats. Even Monty drooped on her shoulder. "Hack says a ship is coming to get us. He's busy as hell now that the Concord ships can be safely searched. So far, the fuckers have a ton of prisoners on each of the bigger ships." She nodded toward the scantily clad men and women. "Hey."

"What is that?" a man asked, pointing at Princess.

"That is Princess Buttercup," Sebastian said proudly. "The greatest soldier on Charybdis Station."

"Now, I must compete with you, Princess," Selene said. She leaned against the wall and eyed the dragon. "I might have to get Draif to help, but we could both use the training."

Alois thought of the pet battles in the backyard. "He's kind of lazy when he's not attacking Concords."

Princess chose that moment to prove his point. He dropped to the floor and exhaled loudly. He laid his head on his arms and was asleep in seconds, snoring loudly.

"He's still the best soldier," Sebastian said, eyes narrowed on the dragon.

About thirty minutes later, Fire's head popped up, and Death looked over his shoulder. "Our ride is here."

Dru stood. "Everyone get moving. Let's get off this ship."

Princess groaned as he stood and started to shrink, hissing the whole time. Alois picked him up and put him on Sebastian's shoulder. Alois's crewmates trudged down the hall, tired and covered in injuries. Mustachio flew above them, singing a sweet, comforting song. The prisoners followed behind them, bunched together, and Death, Sebastian, and Fire walked together at the back. Alois could hear Fire's chatter from the front.

Fasi and Renee ran around a corner and skidded to a stop. "Is everyone alright?" Fasi started patting down Morgan. "Are you hurt?"

"Watch the hands, Lord Admiral," Morgan said with

a laugh. "We're alive. They sent the boss to pick us up?"

"As if I'd let anyone else do it," Fasi said, rolling his eyes. He grinned. "We held our own. It didn't fucking hurt that all our allies came out to help. The Half-Moon Guild may not have been seen, but they saved a lot of people too."

"I didn't know they were here. Well, except for Clara," Dru said.

"No one did," Fasi said, grin widening. "They jumped in when needed, preventing a lot of casualties on our side. I can't wait to merge their tech with ours."

Renee moved past her husband and pushed to the back. "Fire?" She looked the element over.

"Hi! That's me," Fire said, bouncing. "Sebastian freed me, and he said I could come live with him and his mate. He has a daughter named Nina, and she has horns. Have you met her? This is Mustachio. He's really pretty, and Sebastian has his feathers on his stomach. Weird, right? Did you know there's a planet that's mostly deserts? Sebastian said I might be able to visit and run there. I'm hungry. Sebastian said there's this guy named Juniper, and he feeds everyone. He also said there's a woman named Ma who likes to cook. Do you think they'll feed me? I really like cinnamon. Do you like cinnamon?"

Death put a hand over Fire's mouth. "Hello, Renee. This is Fire, and he has agreed to fight with us against the Queen… as long as he isn't made to kill anyone."

The woman struggled to hide her grin. "It's a pleasure to meet you, Fire." She looked at the prisoners. "If you all will follow us, we'll leave this place and get you settled somewhere safe. Know that we will help you reunite with your people, but if you have no one, we will find a home for you. You aren't alone anymore."

"Damn, I love being a Charybdis soldier," Alois said softly. Dru shared a grin with him.

"We're finding a lot of prisoners," Fasi said as he led them to the docking bay. "Everyone is helping search the ships, and several other mercenary groups will continue to pick off any Concords they find in their systems, but we've defeated most of them. There's only a handful left."

"Admiral Sharp got squashed," Selene said in her monotone voice. "I'm disappointed."

"Aww, you didn't get to skewer him?" Fasi patted her shoulder.

"I did not," Selene replied.

"We'll tow the shuttle back to the station," Renee said. "No sense in leaving it behind for scavengers."

"My ship," Dru said. She limped toward the Blue Sparrow. "Mama missed you, baby."

Fasi snorted. "We have blankets and medical supplies inside. Everyone get in."

A familiar figure filled the open door.

"Lerais!" Dru picked up the pace.

"Sweet mama," Lerais said, bounding down the ramp. He picked Dru up and spun her around. "You're okay?"

"Just fine. Let's get home. I have things I want to do," Dru said, eyes full of heat.

Alois and Morgan gagged.

"All aboard," Renee said. "Time to go home."

Sebastian pulled Alois on board the ship and tugged him down the ship's hall straight to Alois's quarters. Sebastian had only seen Alois's room aboard the ship once, but he remembered where it was. The doors opened, and, as soon as the doors closed, Alois grabbed Sebastian, pushing him against the wall, his mouth latching on to Sebastian's. Sebastian wrapped his legs around Alois's hips, and his arms around Alois's neck. He was shaking and couldn't seem to stop.

They fumbled, clumsy and desperate, and ended up sinking to the floor. Alois's hand trembled as he gripped Sebastian's thigh, holding it tight as he pushed into Sebastian's channel. They moved together, frantic, lips whispering to one another.

"Sebastian," Alois said, gasping. "We're alive."

"We're here," Sebastian said, groaning when Alois hit a very nice spot. "We did it. We're together."

"I love you," Alois said, then buried his face in Sebastian's neck, coming hard.

"Love you too," Sebastian said, reaching his own release. "Damn, but I love you so much, Alois."

"It could have gone very wrong," Alois said, breathing heavily. "If the ship had more soldiers on board, if they were spread out better, if Elin hadn't clued us in on the ambushes."

"If Princess Buttercup wasn't with us," Sebastian added, still shaking. "If Fire's binding was stronger." He cupped Alois's face. "I know we needed to do this, but damn, I was *so* scared."

"Me too," Alois said. "There's still Air, Earth, and the Queen to deal with too. After this, she's going to be *really* pissed."

"I wonder what she'll do?" Sebastian said. "She doesn't like to leave her planet, and Air is already ravaging world after world."

"I don't know." Alois held him close, pressing his forehead to Sebastian's. "We're alive now. Nina, Peri, and your stupid bird are safe."

Sebastian laughed. "Mustachio isn't stupid. He helped save the day, you know."

"He flew into battle singing," Alois said. "Stupid."

Sebastian smirked, then got up and headed for the bathroom. "Want to join me in the shower?"

"Do you really need to ask?"

THE DOCKS WERE PACKED when the Blue Sparrow

landed. The Half-Moon ships were docked already, and they patiently waited to be shown their new homes. Hundreds of prisoners had been found on the Concord ships, and they had to go somewhere. Right now, that somewhere was the docks.

Fasi groaned. "This is a mess."

The Blue Sparrow crew ushered the former slaves down the ramp of their ship, Dru in the lead. "Right this way," she called, waving her hand. Mustachio flew out, tail feathers hitting her in the face. "Damn it, Mustachio."

Sebastian smothered his giggles as his bird headed toward Blue Sector.

"Princess!" Leti cried out as he ran to meet them. Princess jumped off Sebastian's shoulder, expanding as he ran to his person. The dragon raised up on his hind legs, towering over Leti, and allowed Leti to hug him tightly. "Are you okay, baby boy? I missed you so much."

"Hey, Leti," Dru said. "We're okay. No one died. Thanks for asking."

Leti blushed, red covering the freckles on his face. "Oh, hey guys. I'm glad everyone's okay."

"He's yours? He's so pretty," Fire said, running to Leti.

"Isn't he?" Leti grinned. "Are you Fire?"

"Yes," the element said. "Where's Ma and Juniper? I'm hungry."

"They're watching the babies and pets at Shae's daycare," Leti said. "We'll get you some food to hold you over until we can properly feed you tonight." He looked at Death. "Verion, can you take him home? He probably needs to process things."

"There are a lot of people that need help right now," Fire said, looking around.

"There are," Fasi said, looking exhausted.

Leti hugged his father-in-law next. "Sebastian, Haroon, and I will take care of getting the Half-Moon people settled in. Morgan, Selene, and Alois will start directing folks to process our new guests. Lerais needs to get Dru to Medical before she falls over."

"I'm fine," Dru said. "Everyone here has injuries."

"No one else got shot," Leti said. "Lerais, get her looked at. Tomorrow morning, we meet at my house for yummy food." Lerais led Dru off, ignoring her protests. Leti looked up at Fasi. "Dad, you and Mom need to go oversee the rest of this operation. Hack and Draif both called me and said it's still going strong. There were a lot of ships in the Concord fleet, and we still need to figure out what to do with those ships and the empty bodies on them."

"Were any of our friends hurt?" Sebastian squeezed Alois's hand, knowing he was worried about Ava and Cordelia in particular.

"Nothing fatal," Leti said.

"Well, Renee, we've been given our orders," Fasi said.

"So, we have," Renee said with a grin. "Alright, everyone. You heard Leti. Let's get to work."

Sebastian kissed Alois and hugged him tightly. "I'll check in with you, and we'll go get Nina tonight."

"Be careful," Alois said. "Leti could still be in danger."

"Someone is trying to hurt Leti?" Clara came to stand next to them. "The Guild Master won't like that. I'll watch his back, Alois."

"Thanks," Alois said. "He has his guards too." Alois looked around. "Wait, where are your guards?"

"I may have snuck out," Leti said, nose wrinkling. "They didn't want me to come."

"Leti, damn it," Maia said, running up to them. "You trying to kill us?" Silas joined her, glaring at Leti.

"Hey there, Maia," Leti said, smiling brightly. "Look at our returning heroes. Oh, and here's Princess. What a surprise." Leti hugged Princess again, and the dragon started to shrink to his traveling size. Leti picked him up and put him on his shoulder. "While we're here, we may as well help out."

"I hate you sometimes," Silas said, sighing. "Then I love you again, but right now, it's all hate."

Sebastian cleared his throat. "The Half-Moon assassins are waiting. Let's get them settled in their new homes." They had put off arriving in order to help pick off ships from the Concord fleet. They had certainly earned a break.

Maia and Silas both scowled, looking scarily alike, and put Leti between them as they headed to the other side of the docks. Clara followed behind them, eyes scanning for danger.

Haroon fell into step beside him. "I can't believe we all made it back."

"Pure luck and Princess Buttercup," Sebastian said.

"He really is the best Charybdis soldier." Haroon grinned, teeth white against his dark skin. For the first time, Sebastian noticed the man didn't look half-bad. He wouldn't have trouble finding company once he finished grieving for Elin.

"Are you checking out my man?" Elin asked, popping up beside him.

He squeaked. "Damn it, Elin." He held his hand to his heart. "No, I am not checking Haroon out. I just noticed he's not bad-looking."

"Wow, that's some compliment," Haroon said dryly.

Elin giggled. "He's a fine man," she said. Her smile faded. "I think it's time I let him move on."

"What are talking about?" Sebastian frowned.

"He has you now. You can watch over him and make sure he doesn't stay in his rut. If I keep popping in and out, I don't think he'll be able to move on," Elin said.

"I don't want you to go," Sebastian said sadly.

"Is she ready to move on?" Haroon asked. He seemed oddly accepting of the idea.

"Yeah," Sebastian said.

"Then it's time," Haroon said. "I love her so damn much. I thought I'd die when she did, but I don't want her to be stuck. I want her to find peace, and I guess that's in the afterlife. I don't know."

"It is," she said. "At least for me."

"Okay," Sebastian said, sniffling. "If you need to leave, we understand."

"I do," she said, smiling. "Before I go, though, I asked around about something."

"Huh? You can talk to other people?"

"I can talk to other dead people, you, and Death. I guess I could talk to the Queen too, but that's not something I want to do," Elin said.

"No," Sebastian said. "That wouldn't be smart."

"So, as I said, I asked around," she continued. "There were all kinds of shamans throughout galactic history. The things I could tell you would seriously freak you out. Anyway, Crellic shamans had spirit guides. Kind of like what I've been to you since we met."

"You'll be my spirit guide?" Sebastian would get to see her then.

"No," she said. "I'd be too tempted to peek in on Haroon."

"She wouldn't be able to rest if she was a spirit guide," Haroon said. "Right?" He shook his head. "I don't even know what I'm saying half the time anymore."

"She agreed with you," Sebastian said, pouting.

"Crellic shamans usually have several spirit guides, but three is a good start," she said. "I've found them for you, and you'll see them soon enough."

"Three? Who are they?"

"You'll see," she said with a grin. She laughed, and her form shimmered with joy. "I almost wish I could stay and see all the things you'll do, but I'm really ready to go now. Tell Haroon I'm sorry and that I love him. Tell him I'll always want the best for him." She didn't wait for his answer. She just disappeared.

"She's gone, hasn't she?" Haroon squeezed his eyes

shut, then opened them again, a determined look on his face.

"She has," Sebastian said. He told Haroon what she'd said. "Why did she say she was sorry?"

"Living wasn't easy on Elin," Haroon said. "She had Roselo's Disease."

Sebastian stopped walking and stared at him in horror. "That's horrible." The disease was incurable and intensely painful.

"She fought for a long time, but she got tired," Haroon said, pulling him until Sebastian was moving again. "There was a nurse that stayed with her while I was gone. I left for a mission and the nurse came over. She was nice, but really young. The nurse fell asleep, and Elin overdosed on her pain meds."

"Haroon," Sebastian said, tears filling his eyes. The Elin he knew was strong and sassy. It was hard to swallow the idea that she killed herself.

"I don't blame her," Haroon said. "The pain she endured was too much even for pain meds to fix. I'm glad she can rest now and isn't suffering anymore, even if I miss her."

Sebastian took his hand. "I understand. She can move on now and so can you. Just not with Jessica."

Haroon laughed roughly. "Not with Jessica." The man jumped when he suddenly had an armful of Leti. Apparently, their conversation hadn't been too private.

"We love you, Haroon, and we're here for you, alright? You're not alone," Leti said, crying softly. He let Haroon go and wiped his eyes.

Silas patted Haroon on the back. "Seriously, man.

You'll never be alone again… whether you like it or not."

They all laughed as Leti sputtered. Then, they approached the line of sleek, small ships. A large group of people stood spread out in front of them. Most were dressed in black and loaded down with weapons. Sebastian wondered how many hidden weapons they had since they had so many visible ones. There were a few normally dressed people mixed in with them, and there was even a baby. A young, dark-skinned woman bounced him in her arms. Baggage was stacked in neat piles behind them all.

A large man with dark-blue hair stepped up, arms crossed. "Clara. Good to see you," he said.

"Bendix," she said, nodding. "Mission was successful."

The man raised a brow. "Fire is on our side now?"

"Yes," she said. "Sebastian here managed to free him." She waved to him. "He can do some crazy shit."

Bendix shrugged. "Okay. The Guild Master will be happy to hear it."

"Wolfe?" Leti ran forward and hugged his friend. Wolfe was slender, young, and very beautiful. He was also mute and, well, *deadly*. "You're finally home again! I can't wait for you to meet Milo."

Sebastian pushed through Maia and Silas to get his own hug. He squeezed the young man tightly. "I'm glad you and your people made it through everything."

"The Crellic System is a fucked-up place," Bendix said. "I led that mission once Wolfe headed back to herd everyone toward Charybdis."

"What's Genarg like?" Leti grabbed the largest bag and started dragging it in the direction of the tram.

"Big fucking jungle with a large pyramid and a shitload of slaves. What are you doing?" Bendix watched Leti drag the bag two whole feet.

"We're going to get you all settled in," Leti said. He huffed and pulled the bag another foot.

"We figured we'd find a hotel or something," Bendix said. "We were just waiting until the docks settled down a bit."

"No hotels for you," Leti said. "We have a nice neighborhood set up. It has several houses and an apartment building, plus it's near Blue Sector, and you'll be close by so I can check in on you all."

Bendix reached down and grabbed the bag from Leti. "A whole neighborhood? Hear that, Pris? You and little Darya get a house."

The woman with the baby grinned. "For real? Hear that, Otto?"

"I was getting around to buying one. Union Station's housing leaves a lot to be desired," Otto said. The man was perfectly average. Average size, average looks, average coloring. Just… average.

"There are a lot for you to choose from here," Leti said. "Beol already paid for everything too, so you just have to pick one out."

"Is this for real?" Pris asked again.

"The Guild Master didn't say he'd done that," Bendix said, shaking his head. "It makes sense though. He's a tough, badass mama bear."

Leti laughed loudly. "Ducks and chickens, I have to

remember to call him that. His face will go all red, and he'll get growly."

Wolfe rolled his eyes and signed. "Why do you like to pick on my brother?"

Leti grinned. "It's fun." He turned toward the Half-Moon assassins. "Everyone grab a bag, and we'll load up the tram. It's time to go home."

ALOIS CLIMBED into bed after showering, exhausted. Sebastian was stretched out on his side already with Nina beside him. Periwinkle lay at the end of the bed, and Mustachio was on a perch in the corner. Alois groaned as his head hit the pillow. "Damn, today was a long day."

"We're alive," Sebastian said. "The Half-Moon assassins are settled into their new homes. All the Concord ships have been cleared, and all the Concord's prisoners are being fed and treated at Medical. Nina, Peri, and Mustachio are home safe and sound."

"Life is good," Alois said. He gripped Sebastian's hand and kissed Nina's head. The little girl was already asleep on her tummy, butt in the air.

The door to their bedroom quietly opened. "Guys? Can I sleep in here with you?" Fire stood at the door, dancing from foot to foot. "I had a dream that the Queen had me again. Sebastian's in here so can I be in here too?"

Sebastian bit his lip and looked at Alois

Alois groaned. "Come on in." Sebastian patted the

bed behind him. At least their bed was huge. "Just think, beautiful, Hack has to sleep with Princess every night."

Fire wiggled into the bed, back to back with Sebastian. "Can I have a cat? I think a cat would be fun to cuddle with at night."

"Go to sleep, Fire," Alois said. "We'll talk about cats in the morning."

15

*A*lois, Dru, and Haroon watched Beck and Pops run around the engineering bay like two kids at Christmas. "Why are we here again?" Dru looked as tired as Alois felt. Even Monty drooped on her shoulder.

It had been a long week, but the rescued Concord prisoners were finally settled. Some chose to stay on Charybdis, some chose to go to Tammol and start over, and some had families to return to. It had been an exhausting time sorting everyone.

"Guys, look at this shielding technology." Beck gripped his tail in one hand and waved a small disc in his other. "My prototypes are completely different. I never would have thought to go this way."

"Your prototypes are fascinating," Hayward said. The older man was Half-Moon's tech master. "I can't believe you created this on your own. It took a full team of engineers years to develop Half-Moon's shield, and their families were being held hostage."

Beck frowned. "Well, that's just not right."

Hayward shrugged. "The old Guild Master was a son of a bitch. You won't see little Beol doing things like that. He's a good boy." The man smiled proudly.

Alois chuckled. "Little Beol. I can't wait to call him that."

"Again," Dru said. "Why are we here?"

"Diplomatic reasons," Bendix said. The big assassin lounged against the wall next to them. "Remember? You're supposed to make sure we all get along."

"Who could be mean to Beck and Pops?" Wolfe signed. The young man watched Pops yelp in excitement as he took a look at Half-Moon's weapon technology.

"Son, call Selene right now. She'll love this," Pops said.

"You'll like her, Hay." Beck ran for his comm.

"They're like kids in a candy store," Otto said, smiling. The man sat on a table in the corner, spinning a dagger in his hand. "Plus, Hayward likes them, so no one would dare hurt the big guys now."

"I'm out," Dru said. "Beck and Pops are having fun, Selene is coming to play, and I need some sleep."

"We promise not to kill any of your people," Bendix said with a smirk.

Dru just patted him on the shoulder as she walked past him. "They're your people now too, Benny-boy."

"Don't call me that," Bendix said with a snarl.

Dru laughed as she left the room.

"Damn," Alois said. "You shouldn't have said that. Now that's all she'll call you."

"Why?" Bendix searched the heavens for divine answers.

"Dru is Dru," Alois said. "It's what she does."

"This is the most fun I've had in months," Beck said, looking closely at a grenade. "Thanks for letting us see all this, Hay."

"No problem, Beck," Hay said with a fond smile. "Beol wants us to help you all as much as we can, and this is easy enough to do."

"Feet still feeling itchy?" Alois watched his friend move back to the blade in front of him. Morgan had described what it could do, and Alois wanted one.

Beck looked up and groaned. "So itchy. I thought maybe someone on Burnished Outpost would be my mate, but no luck. I don't think it's anyone on Charybdis, but there's lots of new folks."

"You'll find him or her soon enough," Alois said.

Haroon grinned. "Maybe it's one of the Half-Moon people."

"I haven't met everyone," Beck said, excitement returning. "That would be good. Ma already wants to adopt them all anyway. She likes your wife, Otto. Ma says Pris is hers now and needs to meet my sisters."

"Pris adores her," Otto said. "She came over last night and cooked us dinner." He eyed Beck. "I may steal her and Pops both. Pris didn't have anyone growing up, and she's soaking it up."

"No need to steal them," Beck said with a smile. "There's enough to go around." He set the blade down.

Selene came in and went straight to the blade. She held it up to the light. "This is mine now."

Alois shared a look with Haroon, and the two men slipped out the door. Alois stretched his arms over his head and moaned as his neck popped. "Want to grab some lunch?"

"Sure," Haroon said. "Then a nap."

"Yes," Alois said, groaning. Both their communicators chimed. "*Fuck*." Alois read the message. "All officers to the conference room. You know, when I became a lieutenant, I never knew how much time officers spent in meetings." They headed toward the tram.

"Seriously," Haroon said. "There are days I wish I had stayed a basic soldier."

"You're too bossy," Alois said. "You were meant for captainship."

"Bossy?"

"That's what your crew says," Alois said, grinning. "You're the bossiest captain out there but also the most practical."

Haroon tilted his head, thinking. "I guess I won't torture them today."

"Such a good captain." Alois snorted. They reached the Lord Admiral's building and entered the conference room. They sat next to Hack and Dru. "What's going on, Hack?"

"No clue," Hack replied. "All I know is Dad is kind of upset and Mom is not happy." A few minutes later, Fasi and Renee came in, and Alois had to admit Fasi looked dire.

"I'll keep this short, everyone," Fasi said. "I know you all are tired from the past week." He looked out at those gathered in the room. "First, Air has attacked another planet. We circulated his picture to everyone months ago, but the element doesn't leave the ship until he's ready to kill."

"Which planet?" Hack asked.

"Elusa in the Radiant System."

Alois gasped. Love's Perfect Match was filmed there. A lot of people lived there. Hmm, a lot of very *wealthy* people. "Let me guess," Alois said. "The galaxy is finally paying attention?"

"Yes," Renee said, hissing the word. "Elusa is a popular place for celebrities and the very rich. The people in the galaxy with the credits are finally noticing."

"That's the real problem," Fasi said. "Some very powerful human purists are using Elusa's devastation as the platform to start a coalition." He pushed a button and a list of names projected above the center of the table. Alois didn't recognize any of them.

"Human purists? The population of Elusa was really diverse," one of Hack's captains pointed out. "The celebrities there weren't all human or even mostly human. It was the same for the wealthy who had homes there."

"This group isn't sympathetic to Air's victims," Renee said, disgust clear in her voice. "They're pointing out the planets that have been targeted are full of non-human races."

"They're *praising* Air's actions!" Fasi exclaimed, growling. The room erupted in noise.

"Seriously?" Haroon looked horrified.

"Why am I not surprised?" Dru shook her head, eyes sad. "All species have factions that hate those that are different. Of course, a group would want to see this all as a good thing."

"These people are very powerful and very wealthy," Renee said. "They've publicly announced their intention to form a coalition to protect human purity. They've also publicly reached out to Air, giving him their approval."

"That's it!" Ava jumped up. "That's what I've been missing. Look at that name at the very top."

"Harrison Goel?" Draif asked for confirmation. He typed the name into his tablet.

"What can we do?" Alois asked.

"What we have been doing," Hack said. "We strengthen our alliances and help others when we can."

"Yes," Fasi said. "I want to beat the shit out of those people, but it's not so easy. All we can do is prepare to protect our system and others as we can."

"What can they do?" Dru asked. "Really. If they form a coalition, what can they actually do?"

"There are no laws to obey in open space," Fasi said solemnly. "Think about our war with the Concords. They weren't breaking any laws, and neither were we."

"They've already reached out to several mercenary groups," Renee said. "Each person on that list has their own private fleet as well. They may be small, but they're a lot better trained than the Concords were."

"If they act like a blunt weapon," Haroon added, "they could bludgeon a world into submission, then take it over or destroy it, just like Air is currently doing."

"Harrison Goel," Draif said. "He has a stronghold on the galactic market for pharmaceuticals."

"He owned the research facility Dr. Morrick worked at," Ava said. "What if the person Morrick's bosses worked for wasn't Life or Admiral Sharp? What if the Concords were just a weapon, not the top of the chain of command?"

"The first two worlds were vacation spots," Haroon said. "We need the guest lists. What if they had competition there?"

"What about Icewilde?" Dru looked thoughtful. "Tammol and Icewilde have a lot in common. Decimating non-human worlds sounds like a human purist thing to do. The Concords wanted to set up base on Tammol, but they sure as shit enjoyed killing most of the population."

"Won't destroying non-human worlds impact their businesses? The men and women listed here are actively involved in a lot of different sectors of the galactic economy," Draif said. He pulled his tablet out. "If their money is threatened, it would sure as shit make them unhappy."

"I don't know," Fasi said, intrigued. "Draif, will you look into all this and write a report for me? We've been focusing on the Queen and the Concords. The thought that we may have another enemy out there is worrisome."

"I will," he said, eyes glued to his tablet. "The second guy on the list deals in medical products, and

Charybdis Station is a competitor of his. Hmm." He looked up. "I wonder if they want to use this purity bullshit for their own gains."

"You mean destroy Charybdis, or another non-human world, because it's full of non-humans, but also take advantage of the fall of their competitors?" Renee gave a mock gasp. "They wouldn't stoop that low, would they?"

"Get me that report, Draif," Fasi said. "I thought this was stalled with the end of the Concords."

"What about Air and the Queen?" Hack asked.

"Air needs to be taken out. He's killed billions," Fasi said. "Beol is on his tail, but until we get a shot at him, we're at an impasse. The Queen is on Genarg, and from what we know, she doesn't leave the planet."

"We focus on Air and then move on from there," Renee said. "We'll also reach out to our allies to prepare for whatever this coalition has planned."

ALOIS AND HAROON finally made it home. After the conference, any peace they felt had disappeared, and Alois had insisted Haroon come eat lunch at his house rather than go home to an empty apartment. Alois opened the door and walked in. He came to a stop and stared at Sebastian. His mate was in the center of the living room, floating. A silvery white light surrounded him. The colors didn't match any of his tattoos, so Alois figured he was using the air element.

Fire sat on the couch with Nina on his lap. Peri sat

next to him, and Mustachio perched on the back of the couch. Fire shoved a handful of cinnamon candy in his mouth, while Nina chewed on her fist. Death sat in a chair next to the window. His head rested on his fist, face thoughtful. Everyone's eyes were trained on Sebastian.

"Hey," Alois said, moving slowly. He didn't want to startle Sebastian and make him fall.

Fire turned to look at him, waving wildly. "Hi, guys. Sebastian met one of his new spirit guides today. He's an old Crell named Tell." Fire cackled. "Crell named Tell."

"Okay?" Haroon sat on the couch with Fire and watched Sebastian. "So, there's a guy named Tell."

"Yes," Death said. "He's one of the shamans that trained the Queen. He agreed to become Sebastian's spirit guide so that he can *properly* train him. Sebastian is the last Crellic shaman."

"Properly, huh? Is someone jealous?" Alois asked, smirking.

Death blew a raspberry and Alois laughed. He plucked Nina up and kissed her cheeks. His little girl giggled and pressed sloppy wet kisses on his face. He sat next to Peri, and his dog snuggled up with him. "Is he going to be good enough to fight the Queen?"

"No," Fire said, shaking his head. "No way." He stuffed another handful of candy in his mouth and chewed furiously.

"Sebastian has a lot of talent, but he just doesn't have the experience or knowledge that the Queen has. This"—Death waved at Sebastian—"has nothing to do with the Queen. It's about being a Crellic shaman. The more he knows, the better he can help everyone around him."

"That's not a bad thing," Haroon said. He pulled a blanket from the back of the couch and curled up, watching Sebastian sleepily.

"No," Alois said. "It's not a bad thing."

He thought of Sebastian's joy at helping the crops in the gardens and his disgust at killing Leti's would-be assassin. There were a lot of ways to help Charybdis Station, and Alois had a feeling Sebastian wasn't going to be on the front lines.

He'd better not be, Alois thought with a scowl.

16

THREE MONTHS LATER

Tell paced in front of the couch Sebastian sat on with Nina and Fire. The man was in constant movement. When they'd first met, Sebastian thought the old Crell was extremely intimidating. He was well over seven feet tall with wild white hair, blue skin, and curling tusks protruding from the corners of his mouth. His shape was far more solid than Elin's had been.

Now, though, Sebastian knew the man was a big softie. He was so encouraging and always had a kind word for Sebastian, even when he fucked up big time. He had also helped Sebastian and Leti on a side project. Wyatt, Orsla, and Death needed help in figuring out a permanent solution to Water and Life. Tell had gladly offered his assistance through Sebastian. Tell and Leti offered a unique perspective on the artifacts.

"We checked the crops and purified the grass and air," Tell said, making another turn. "We strengthened the core of the Station. What else is tugging at you, Sebastian?"

Mustachio chittered from his cage where he was eating breakfast.

Sebastian nibbled his lip, then closed his eyes, easily slipping into the spirit world. After three months, he didn't need Mustachio's song, but he still found comfort in his bird's closeness. Sebastian spread out across the station, looking for a tug like Tell had taught him. He searched and searched, then found it.

"Something isn't right at the docks," he said. "Someone's there that shouldn't be."

"Good," Tell said. "What isn't right about this person?"

"Their heart isn't with Charybdis," Sebastian said. "Does that even make sense?"

"Their heart is bad," Fire said, shrugging. "They want to do bad things on Charybdis?"

"Yes," Sebastian said, eyes popping open. "I need to call Alois."

"Wait," Tell said. "We need to learn as much as we can about this person so that your mate can find him."

"Oh, yeah." Sebastian closed his eyes again and focused on the person with the bad heart. "It's a human woman with brown hair and blue eyes. She's just arrived on a ship. It's a small, personal shuttle. She came from… Vextonar." He opened his eyes. "I still don't know what her intentions are, but that's where Leti's from, and it's dominated by human purists."

"That should be enough for Alois and the others to find her," Tell said. "Message him now."

Sebastian quickly typed the message and sent it to both Alois and Hack. He breathed a sigh of relief when they both replied back to him quickly. "They're going to look into it."

"Excellent job, Sebastian," Tell said. "You have a lot of potential, but you need to work on focusing. Let's do some meditation exercises, then I'll leave you to work on your translations."

"Sure," Sebastian said, settling into the middle of the floor. He looked at Fire. "You don't have to stay, Fire."

"It's Nina cuddling time," Fire said, shrugging.

Sebastian hid his frown. He really liked Fire, but the element hadn't strayed far from either his or Death's side since he was freed. Fire had nightmares each night and was so damn scared all the time. The Queen had to go.

"Okay. Remember to eat something more than candy," Sebastian said, ignoring the face Fire made at him. He closed his eyes and entered the spirit world. Time to focus.

***

Sebastian, Fire, and Nina were at Leti's house when Alois found them. Grandpa Moses and Fire were in the backyard, playing with the kids, Wobble, Trixie, and Princess. Sebastian sat at his desk, Abbot in his lap, working on a translation for Dr. Chopra. Leti sat in the window seat, reading a book, while Pepper stumbled around the room, new to walking. Milo slept in a little bassinet in the corner.

Hack and Alois both came in and grabbed chairs far apart from one another. Both wore matching grins. Leti looked up, eyeing the men. "Did Alois finally forgive you?" he asked Hack.

Alois scowled. "No. I'm not here *with* him. We both just happened to be coming here."

Hack gave Alois an imploring look. "Come on, Alois. It's been a month."

"You got my girl pregnant, Hack!"

"Stop saying that," Hack said with a groan. Sebastian and Leti looked at each other, lips pressed tight to smother their laughter.

"Fine. *Your* dog got Periwinkle pregnant. She's too young to be a mama," Alois said, growling.

"I didn't realize Gravy wasn't fixed," Hack said. "He'll be a good daddy dog. I promise."

"They're in the backyard now," Leti said, looking out the window. "Aww, they're all cuddled up together."

"She's too young!" Alois's face was as red as his scales.

"The vendor said she was alright to breed at five months," Sebastian said. "That seems young in comparison to other canine species, but it's normal for a Siren dog, and Peri is a little over six months old now."

"She's having three puppies, Sebastian. That's a lot of responsibility," Alois said. He pointed at Hack. "He should have made Gravy behave." Sebastian couldn't help it. He met Leti's eyes again, and the two of them started laughing. "Laugh it up," Alois said, sniffing. "I'm the one who has to find homes for my three grandpuppies."

"I'll help," Hack said. "They're my grandpuppies too."

Alois glared at him. "Damn right they are! You had best take responsibility, Hack."

"I will. I will," Hack said. "We have all of Blue Solace to choose from. What about Haroon?"

Alois thought for a minute. "I like that." He sighed and looked back at Hack. "I guess I can forgive you since we're going to be grandparents together."

"Thanks, man. I'll get Gravy fixed soon," Hack said.

"Wait," Leti said. "If that happens, we don't get any more puppies."

"Okay, okay," Sebastian said, holding his hands up. "Let's shelf that discussion for now." He got up and set Abbot on the floor. The rabbit hopped over to Pepper, and the little girl giggled as she plopped to her butt to play with him. Sebastian sat in Alois's lap and kissed his cheek. "What happened with the woman at the docks?"

"Oh yeah," Leti said. "Did you guys find her?"

"We did," Hack said, leaning back. "You are a treasure, Sebastian. You know that, right?"

"Sebastian the Phenomenal," Leti said, smugly. "*My* friend."

Alois hugged him. "The woman works for the new coalition, Humans First."

"Eww," Leti said, nose wrinkling. Sebastian fully agreed with him.

"She was here to locate Life and Water's artifacts," Hack said. "Apparently, they want to put them to use."

"Damn it," Sebastian said. "Are they working for the Queen? We just got rid of the Concords."

"As far as we can tell, they aren't working for or with her," Hack said. "Life and Water have both been mentioned in the media because of the noticeable damage they've caused alongside the Concords. It wouldn't be hard to trace them here."

"I suspect we just haven't found the connection between them yet," Sebastian said.

"How did this woman know to look for the artifacts?" Leti didn't look happy. "That's not common knowledge, Hack."

"Fuck. I didn't think about that," Hack said. "Let me talk to Dad about it. I'll be back for dinner, baby." He got up and gave Leti a kiss, then left the room. Leti watched him go, eyes hot. His tiny growl made Sebastian laugh again.

"Oh gods, you are adorable." He wiped his eyes. "So, who all knew about the artifacts? We haven't really kept it a secret," Sebastian said.

"They would have had to hear about it from either someone at Charybdis Station or one of our allies," Leti said. "It wouldn't have been hard to get that information, but we need to know their connection."

"True," Alois said. He kissed Sebastian's nose. "We wouldn't have noticed anything off about the woman. She was a complete professional. Fuck, we had to push at her hard to get her to admit to being there for anything other than a vacation. Thank you, Sebastian the Phenomenal."

Sebastian blushed. "Tell is the one we should thank. Something was tugging me to the docks, but I didn't really focus on it until he told me to."

"How's it going with him?" Leti got up when Milo whimpered. The smell in the air told everyone it was diaper-changing time.

"Great," Sebastian said. "He's so sweet. I really wish you all could meet him. Death still sits in on my lessons as often as he can, but he never talks to spirits. Says he doesn't want to scare them," Sebastian shrugged. "Between the two of them, I've learned a lot of ways to help Charybdis."

"I'm so proud of you, beautiful," Alois said, kissing him softly. His comm chimed, and Sebastian's mate groaned. He looked down. "Shit. They want the both of us in the conference room, Seb. Fire too."

"I'll watch Nina," Leti said. "Grandpa Moses is here, and Shae's coming over for lunch in about fifteen minutes, so the babies shouldn't take over the house today."

"They'll save that for tomorrow," Sebastian said, smiling. "I'll go get them."

He left Leti and Alois arguing about spaying and neutering Gravy and Peri. He slipped out the backdoor. Fire had Nina strapped to his chest, facing the front. She waved her legs and arms excitedly, while Fire, Trixie, and Wobble both chased a giggling Sami around the yard. Grandpa Moses sat in a chair, sleeping, and

Princess lounged in the hammock with Stardust curled up on his scaled stomach.

"Where's Periwinkle?" He looked around and finally spied her. At six months old, she was huge, even bigger than Gravy. The two dogs curled together on a few large pillow seats. Gravy rested his huge head over her, occasionally leaning up to lick Peri's snout. Sebastian sighed. Alois's baby was in love. Sebastian shook his head, then looked back to Fire. "Hey, bud. We need to go talk to the Lord Admiral."

"Fasi and Renee! I love them," Fire said. He grabbed Sami up and tickled him. The little boy shrieked with laughter. "Can we bring Nina? Please? I'll hold her really good." They walked back to Leti's office.

"Leti said he would watch her," Sebastian said. Leti grabbed Sami and tossed him in the air. The boy was growing fast, and Leti wouldn't be able to do that much longer.

"I can watch her," Fire said, pouting. "Please, please, please." His big, fiery eyes pleaded with both Leti and Sebastian.

"Okay," Sebastian said, shaking his head. Fire was too sweet.

Leti patted Fire's cheek. "Love you, Fire. Remember, we're having dinner at my house tonight."

"Is Ma or Juniper cooking?" Fire eyed him suspiciously.

Leti stomped his foot. "My cooking is just fine."

"Ma or Juniper?"

"Ma," Leti said with a sigh.

"Okay," Fire said happily. He ran out the door.

Alois laughed and followed him. Sebastian shared an amused look with Leti, then followed them at a more sedate pace. They jumped on the tram, walking quickly, and entered the conference room right on time. Not a lot of people were there. Dru and her crew, along with the rest of Blue Solace, and Death sat beside Morgan and Lerais. Bendix, Hack, and the rest of the generals sat along one side of the table. No other officers were present. Sebastian nibbled his lip. This couldn't be good.

Fasi stood at the front of the room, and Fire went right to him. Fasi opened his arms, and the playful element jumped into the hug, somehow managing not to squish Nina.

"Hey there, son," Fasi said, squeezing Fire tightly. Renee poked her husband's side so she could get her own hug. It looked so strange to have the middle-aged couple treating the old man like a child. It was Fire though. As old as his body was, as old as his essence was, he was a young soul.

Fasi turned back to the room. "Alright, everyone. We have a couple of items of news, and we don't want it spread about. First, thanks to Sebastian, we found a spy sent to us by Humans First. She has been charged with espionage and will be detained in our prison."

"It's starting, then," Draif said. The young captain had thoroughly researched each founding member of Humans First and noticed they all had non-human competition for the products or services they sold. They also were heavily connected to the galactic economy. Sebastian agreed with Draif that this would be Humans First's weak spot.

"It is," Fasi said. "However, we have some good news too." He gestured to Wyatt.

Death's son stood and waved to the room. "Hey. We just wanted to let you know that we have found a way to permanently destroy Life and Water. Their essences will be dispersed, and the artifacts destroyed."

"Yes," Hack said, raising his fists. "Leti said you guys were close."

"It'll take some time, but Leti, Orsla, and I will get started on it right away," Wyatt said.

Sebastian frowned. Did they not want to work with him?

Fasi cleared his throat. "Our next bit of news is good too. Beol found Air."

The whole room cheered. The Queen's element had devastated another planet since Elusa. "The bad news," Renee said, "is that Air is untouchable at the moment." She looked at Sebastian, Fire, and Death. "Beol says he stays in an airy form? It's hard to describe."

Death winced. "I didn't even think about that. Life and I could never change our forms, so it's easy to forget the others can do that." He looked at Fire. "Do you want to demonstrate?"

Fire unstrapped Nina and handed her to Alois. "Sure. It's fun." He went to the front of the room and waved at them all. They all waved back. He grinned, then his body changed. Flames twirled around him until his body was gone and all that was left was a swirling blaze and a pile of ashes. The blaze moved across the front of the room, back and forth. Then it stopped, and the flames faded until Fire stood there again, naked. Everyone stared at Fire in amazement. Sheiria snickered.

"You're naked, Fire." Sebastian jumped up and grabbed Hack's coat from the back of his chair. He wrapped it around Fire's hips.

"Oops," Fire said, biting his lips. "I forgot clothes are important."

"Yes, they are," Sebastian said, blushing and heading back to his seat.

"I'm cold," Fire said with a pout. Renee hugged Fire and wrapped Fasi's coat around him. She hugged him tightly, and he pressed his face against her neck.

"You're welcome," Hack said dryly as Sebastian passed him. "For lending you my coat." Sebastian rolled his eyes and kicked Hack's foot.

"Life and Water were both killed," Death said. "Air is frightened, and the elemental form is much harder to hurt than our bodies."

"Beol can't kill him," Selene said. "A poison would have no effect on him right now."

"Exactly," Fasi said. Fire bounced back to Sebastian and sat on him until he scooched over, sharing his chair. Fire wrapped his arms around Sebastian and settled his head on his shoulder.

"There was a reason Life and I were the ones to hunt wayward elements," Death said. "I can manipulate his form to some degree, and Life could play with his mind."

Fasi looked grim. "We thought you might say that.

We're reluctantly asking you to go help Beol deal with Air. The devastation the element is causing must stop."

Death nodded. "Of course." He looked at Sebastian and Fire. "I might need some help."

"I'll go," Fire said in a small voice. His body trembled. "I can burn him and make him steam."

"If Fire goes, I have to go," Sebastian said, eyes finding Alois. He reached his hand out to his mate. "I can't let the Queen get him again. He's our family now."

If they left now, they'd miss the date they had set for their wedding. They'd miss Peri's puppies being born. They'd miss seeing Nina for another month. Fire's wet tears on Sebastian's neck convinced him it was the right thing to do.

Alois reached out and took his hand. "Absolutely. You go, I go."

"The Blue Sparrow is repaired and ready for flight," Dru said. "We're the fastest ship in Hack's fleet."

"I'll take care of Nina," Selene said. "Xu likes babies, so he'll help too." Her son was a sweet boy and very good with babies.

"I'll be there for our grandpuppies," Hack said, patting Alois's shoulder.

"Juniper and I will take care of the date change for your wedding," Ava said. "You *will* have your dream wedding, Sebastian."

"When do we leave?" Sebastian squeezed Alois's hand and kissed the side of Fire's head. They would take care of Air. It was time to end this.

17

SILVERLIGHT SYSTEM

A couple of weeks later and Alois missed his Nina desperately. Seeing her on the vid-screen was completely different than holding her in his arms. Plus, Peri had even had her puppies. The little fluff balls were the cutest things Alois had ever seen, and he wanted to be there to pet them. Hack had sent him a picture of Gravy holding one down and licking it clean while Peri nursed the other two. Alois wanted to go home, damn it.

He loved his crew members, but everyone was a little miserable. Quinn missed Cordelia. Rune had insisted on coming since Dru didn't have an official medic, and he was slowly pining away for Silas. Worst of all, Morgan's hourly calls home to Wyatt were starting to gross everyone out. They were pathetic former mercenaries turned homebodies.

"Alois, can I tell you something?" Sebastian asked, pulling him out of his misery. Alois jumped out of the chair and went to his mate. He cupped Sebastian's cheek and watched him chew on his lip. What the hell had Sebastian so nervous?

"Are you unhappy with the ship? Our room is a little small, but it's not horrible." Alois had to admit it was a big change from their home.

"No," Sebastian said. "Our room is just fine, and Mustachio and Fire like it too." Mustachio currently flew up and down the hallway of the ship, dipping to ruffle the hair of anyone below him. Alois grinned when he heard another crewmate yell. Yeah, that time it was Hazel.

"It's nice, but I like Charybdis more," Fire said. "I want to go home." The old man curled up in a large, well-padded chair next to the window. His knees were pulled up under his chin, and his big, fiery eyes were sad.

"We'll be home soon enough," Alois said, then looked back at Sebastian. "What's wrong, beautiful?"

"My parents have been calling me ever since Ava paid my debt and freed me," Sebastian said.

Alois growled. He wasn't a fan of Sebastian's parents. "I thought that might be what all those rejected calls were about. What do they want?"

"I haven't answered," Sebastian said, nibbling his lips. "I have two sisters. They were seven or eight when I was sold."

"Do you want to check on them?"

"I should," Sebastian said. "I've been avoiding everything to do with my parents, but I kind of want to know how Sai and Salla are doing. They're twins."

"Sebastian, Sai, and Salla," Alois said. "Are we going to name our kids something with an S?"

Sebastian made a face. "Shut it, honey bear."

"Honey bear?"

"Renee and Ma call their men all kinds of pet names," Sebastian said. "I'm trying to find one to fit you."

"It's not honey bear."

"I like honey," Fire said, staring out at the stars. "Honey bear."

Sebastian covered his mouth, his eyes dancing with laughter.

Alois sighed. "I'm honey bear now, aren't I?"

Sebastian silently nodded. When he could speak again, Sebastian uncovered his mouth and cleared his throat. "Anyway, they all live on Union Station, and I know we'll be stopping there to resupply at some point. I kind of want to see my sisters."

"I think that's a good idea," Alois said. "I'll go with you and try not to kill your parents."

Sebastian's smile was both sad and grateful. "I don't know if I could do this without you."

"You could," Alois said honestly. "You're stronger than you think, but you don't have to do it alone because I'm with you."

"Me too," Fire said, looking away from the window. "I want to meet your sisters. Are they nice? Do they like chocolate squirrels. I didn't think I would, but Leti is right. They're the best."

"I don't know, Fire," Sebastian said. "I want to find out though." His comm chimed and he sighed. "Perfect timing." He accepted the call, and a woman's face popped up. Alois didn't like her. She looked snooty.

"Oh, you answered," she said in surprise. "Sebastian. It's so good to see you."

"Yeah," Sebastian said. "So good. Anyway, how are Sai and Salla?" Alois pulled him into his arms. His body was stiff and trembling.

"They're fine," the woman said, eyes on Alois. "Who's that man with you?"

"My life-mate," Sebastian said. "Alois, this is Carleen, my mom."

"It's nice to meet you," Carleen said, smiling hesitantly. "I'm glad Sebastian found someone to take care of him."

"He doesn't need me to take care of him," Alois said. "Your son is one of the strongest people I know."

"Sure," Carleen said, nodding. "Anyway, Sebastian, your father and I wanted to check up on you now that you're on your own. I guess you aren't near Union Station anymore since you took up with those mercenaries."

"Actually, we'll be there in a few days to resupply," Sebastian said. "I thought I'd come by to see Sai and Salla."

"That would be perfect," Carleen said, relief filling her eyes. Alois frowned. Something wasn't right here. "Come right to the house when you arrive. I'll send you our new address."

Fire bounced beside them on the bed, waving at the woman. "Oh, this is..." Alois cut Sebastian's introduction off. "I'll make sure he gets there,

Carleen." He gently shoved Fire out of the woman's view.

"One other thing," Sebastian said, pinching Alois's leg. "Do you have any of Gramma's stuff? I was thinking about her the other day, and I'd like to have something of hers to give to our daughter if it's possible."

"Daughter?" Carleen's face lit up. "Is she with you?" Alois didn't like the eagerness in her voice. Something was definitely not right.

"No," Sebastian said. "We had to leave her behind for this mission."

"Mission? Oh, never mind," Carleen said. "I don't want to know. Just come by the house when you arrive. Your mate should probably stay on the ship. I don't know how your father will react to him." She smiled a sickly sweet, fake smile. "I hope you understand, Alois."

"Of course," Alois said.

Sebastian ended the call and turned in his arms, eyes questioning. "You aren't going with me?"

"Why didn't you introduce me?" Fire pouted.

"Alright, guys. Something is wrong with that woman," Alois said.

"Yeah," Sebastian said. "She's a bitch that sold her child."

"She seems really eager to get her hands on you," Alois said. "A little too eager. I'm going to ask Draif to look into your parents' finances real quick." He shot off a message to Draif, then looked at Fire. "I didn't want her to know about you in case she's up to something. We don't want you to get hurt."

"Okay," Fire said, shrugging. "I'm going with you though. I won't let anyone hurt Sebastian either." He pulled Sebastian and Alois into a hug. "You're the best, honey bear." He let them go and bounced out the door.

Alois heard Dru yell. "Damn it, Mustachio."

"I like your bird now," Alois said.

"That was fast," Sebastian said. "It's only been several months now."

Alois was about to respond when Sebastian's face grew white, and his mouth dropped open. His eyes were fixed on the door. Alois turned to look. There was nothing there.

"What's wrong, beautiful?" Alois asked. He pushed Sebastian behind him and faced the empty door.

"Gramma?" Sebastian's voice was barely more than a croak.

"Your dead Gramma?" Alois's head ached. Seeing spirits was fucked up.

"Yes," Sebastian said, then grinned. "She's my second spirit guide." He started bouncing behind Alois. "She said you're hot."

"Well..." Alois stood straighter. "She seems like a nice woman."

Sebastian laughed and moved around him. His laughter stopped, and his face grew red with anger. Alois had never seen Sebastian mad before, but damn, his mate was pissed. Alois's comm chimed, and he looked at the message. Draif had checked into Sebastian's parents, and they were covered in fucking debt again. Shit.

"Gramma says Mom and Dad are in debt again," Sebastian said.

"Draif just messaged me about that," Alois said. "Shit. What are they planning?"

"Gramma says they were planning on selling Sai and Salla. They're fifteen, and one of the guys my parents owe is a serious perv and wants them," Sebastian said.

"Not happening," Alois said. "We get there in two days, and we'll save them."

"Oh, that's not all," Sebastian said. "Since we talked, Mom and Dad now plan to sell me again too. My old boss misses me."

"Those fucking pieces of shit!" Alois yelled.

"Uh, you guys okay in here?" Dru poked her head in. Monty perched on her shoulder and tilted his head, watching them.

"Sebastian's dead Gramma just told us his parents plan to sell him again along with his younger sisters," Alois said, teeth gritted.

"His dead… Never mind. Okay," Dru said, stepping into the room. "Obviously, that's not going to happen. What do we do?"

"We?" Sebastian looked at Dru, confused.

"Sebastian," Dru said. "Haven't you figured it out yet? We're family, and we stick the fuck together."

"Oh," Sebastian said, eyes watering. "Gramma really likes you, Dru."

"She sounds like a wise woman," Dru said. "Now, what the fuck do we do? Obviously, we can keep them from selling Sebastian, but what about his sisters? How old are they?"

"Fifteen," Alois said.

"Let me get Ava on it," Dru said. "We can just take them and sort it out later. Ava has a gift for smoothing our fuck-ups out."

"We could just pay them for the girls," Alois said. Their safety was more important than his own pride.

"No," Sebastian said. "I refuse to let those assholes benefit from hurting Sai and Salla." He tilted his head, clearly listening to his grandmother. "Gramma says that Sai found her life-mate already, and he'll need to come with us. They're in love and plan to marry in a few years, which is another reason my parents are doing all this now."

"She's fifteen," Alois said. "That's way too young to have a life-mate."

"Gramma says you just try to stop it." Sebastian snorted. "What would you have done if you met me when you were fifteen?"

"Yeah, Alois," Dru said, smirking. "What would you have done at fifteen?"

"We'd have ten kids by now," Alois said, grumbling.

Sebastian laughed at him but cuddled into his side. "Gramma says Sai is a science freak like Nina. She has a good head on her shoulders and plans on going to college. She'll marry her beau, but they won't be popping out babies right away." He listened for a second. "She says they have two guinea pigs and a cat too."

"Okay. How do we make this happen?" Dru stroked

the hilt of her phaser. "Wait. The Lord Admiral said it just the other day. No one governs the stars. Whatever happens, happens."

"So? We'll be on Union Station, and until the age of eighteen, children belong to the parents there. They can do whatever they want with their children," Sebastian said.

"What if we had a few stowaways like Leti and Draif? We wouldn't know about them until we were off planet," Dru said. "We simply wouldn't have the time to turn around and return them."

"Ava could explain everything to Union Station," Alois said, grinning. "Smooth things over. We probably couldn't get back to Union Station until they were eighteen though."

"We *are* really busy people," Dru said, nodding.

"What's the mate's name?" Alois looked around the room. "Gramma?"

Sebastian smiled wide. "She says she loves that you call her Gramma. His name is Lorry Philbert."

"Philbert?" Dru snickered. "She'll be stuck with that name. Poor Sai."

"Let's give Lorry a call," Alois said. "We'll arrange everything, and then Sebastian and I will go visit to distract the assholes."

"I'm coming too," Fire said, and Alois yelled in a very manly fashion.

"Fuck! Where were you? I didn't even hear you come in." Alois held a hand to his chest.

"I sneaked," Fire said. "I wanted to know what was wrong, so I eavesdropped. Hi, Gramma!" He waved toward a spot near the window. "Did Alois's squeal scare you?"

"I didn't squeal," Alois said.

"No, honey bear," Sebastian said. "You didn't squeal at all."

PLANET UNION STATION, SILVERLIGHT SYSTEM

"Now, sweetheart, Lorry is a good boy, but he's very young," Gramma said. "Tell your mate not to startle him."

"Startle him? Really?" Sebastian had a feeling Sai's mate was a baby deer or something. When they called Lorry's house yesterday, his dad had answered. Since time was running out and they arrived in the morning, Dru had taken Gramma's advice and told the Betonize man everything. Luckily, Valentine Philbert was a good man. He was a single parent and worked in one of the factories on Union Station.

"Just be nice," Gramma said. "I'm glad Dru talked Lorry's dad into coming too. They don't have a lot, but he's a good person. He'll be a good worker for your station. Lord knows that place needs more than soldiers." Gramma's bright form moved around the room. She was just as he remembered her – short, chubby, and sassy.

"How do you know he's a good man?" Sebastian watched her suspiciously.

"I've been keeping an eye on my grandbabies," the old woman said, indignant. "It's my job, sweetheart."

"They should be here in two hours," Dru said, pacing the floor of the small cargo bay.

"Calm down, sweet mama," Lerais said. "Val seems like a sensible guy. He'll get them here while Sebastian and Alois distract the assholes."

"Why do our missions always get weird? Somehow, we seem to end up with more people than we start with," Dru said. Lerais just pulled her to him and kissed her until she stilled.

"Ready to do this, beautiful?" Alois held his hand, and Sebastian was so damn happy to have him here. Sebastian knew he *was* strong, but doing this alone would be horrible.

"I'm ready." He looked to his right. "Fire, are you sure you want to come?"

"Yep," Fire said. "Death's coming too. We're your friends."

"Death?" Alois looked around. "Why is he coming?"

"Right behind you, Alois," Death said, laughter in his voice. Alois squealed and jumped, making everyone laugh.

"Damn it, Morrick." Alois spun around, glaring at their friend.

"Anyway," Death said, smirking. "I'm coming to make sure Fire doesn't do anything stupid. Plus, he's right. We're your friends. Your crew has to be here to deal with supplies and meet with Sebastian's sisters, so we'll watch your backs this time."

"Good man," Dru said, punching Death's arm. "Okay. You guys get going. We'll have the stowaways settled in by the time you get back."

Sebastian took a deep breath and pulled Alois down the ramp. He didn't want to see his parents, but life wasn't always fair. He had to think about Sai and Salla. They loaded into a shuttle and rode out of the spaceport. His parents' new house was in the upper city. It was in a nice neighborhood, which definitely explained their new debt since neither of his parents could keep a steady job.

Sebastian closed his eyes and felt the planet around him. Death had been right when he said a planet felt a lot different from Charybdis Station. There was a deep strength and beauty to the planet. Even with the surface mostly covered in cities, the planet still had a vibe all its own.

"You feel it?" Fire lay his head on Sebastian's shoulder.

"Yeah. You?"

"Yep," Fire said. "I like planets, but Charybdis Station is home now, so it's the best."

"I miss it too," Sebastian said. They pulled up to his parents' neighborhood, and the car stopped. Despite Alois's protests, they had decided Sebastian would go in alone. He wanted to see what his parents had planned. Alois and the others would be backup.

"Be careful, beautiful," Alois said.

"I'll keep your honey bear safe, Seb," Fire said and kissed his cheek.

Sebastian laughed when Alois growled. "Thanks, Fire. I'll leave my communicator activated. You guys can come save the day if my parents get too weird," Sebastian said. He leaned up and kissed Alois. The taste of his mate always made him feel safe. He turned and walked toward their house before he could change his mind.

Carleen and Shaine Dolarnio answered the door together. They looked like nice people, well-dressed and pleasant looking. Sebastian knew them though.

"Sebastian, darling," his mom said and pulled him into a hug.

His dad shut the door behind them and patted his back. "It's just so wonderful to see you, son." Sebastian wanted to throw up. Fasi and Pops could call him *son*. His bio dad could eat shit. His father's wide grin would look better with Alois's fist in it. "I'll be right back. We found some of my mother's things for you."

He went upstairs, and Sebastian turned to his mom. He forced a smile. "Hey. I guess Sai and Salla are in school right now."

"Yes," Carleen said, pulling him farther into the house. "They'll be back for dinner though." She looked around the kitchen. "Their cat is around here somewhere, but I haven't seen it this morning. You'll probably like the rabid creature." She invited him to sit with her at the table. "I wish your daughter was here. It would make things easier."

"What do you mean?"

"Sebastian, darling, your father and I have made some bad choices recently. There are some very mean men who want to hurt us." She patted his hand and looked at him earnestly. "You don't want us to be hurt, do you? If we're dead, what would happen to Sai and Salla?"

"What do you want?" Sebastian knew Alois and the others heard every word coming from her. They were there for him and wouldn't let what he knew was coming happen.

"Qeavan Mcada wants you back," she said, then sighed. "It hurts so much to have you with us again only to lose you."

"He's offered to pay your debts?"

"Well, most of them," Carleen said. "If your daughter was here, we could sell her to pay the rest of it. Do you think Charybdis Station will send her to us once you're indentured?"

"What makes you think I would agree to this?" Sebastian couldn't believe she was so nonchalant about this. Last time, they had completely taken him by surprise.

"Darling, you won't have a choice," she said. He felt a band snap around his neck from behind.

"Qeavan here brought a collar," his dad said. "It's a nice little gadget that can kill you in an instant. I suggest you listen to him."

Sebastian slowly turned around. Qeavan and his usual guards stood next to his father. The sleazy bastard smiled brightly. "So nice to see you again, Sebastian. We have a lot of customers asking about our

Wednesday night special. They'll be pleased that you're back."

He turned back to the woman that birthed him. "They won't send my daughter to you. Alois is her father, and even if he wasn't able to care for her, my friends and family would."

"Family? We're your family," Carleen said. "A mercenary station is no place for a baby."

"You are not my family," Sebastian said. "You two are pieces of garbage that have no right to me, my daughter, or my sisters."

"Sebastian, don't talk to your mother that way," Shaine said.

"My mothers are Renee Juren and Ma Brackenstone," he said. "My fathers are Fasi Juren and Pops Brackenstone. The two of you are nothing to me."

Carleen looked dumbfounded, but Shaine just shrugged. "It doesn't matter what you think. You're going with Qeavan and the twins will go to Drial. We'll try to get custody of the baby later. There are a lot of people who would pay for a baby."

"I can set you up with some buyers," Qeavan said. "Let me know when you get her."

"This is illegal," Sebastian said. "I could defend myself and not face charges."

"I would love for you to try," Qeavan said, laughing. "My guards here missed you too, and you know they like to punish you."

"Choose your path, sweetheart," Gramma said. "They deserve to die."

"What's my other option?" He looked at her. She was one pissed spirit.

"What? You don't have any other options," Carleen said.

"We have the recordings because of your communicator," Gramma said. She looked at him. "This is a very important choice, sweetheart. Neither choice is really evil, but it will shape who you are as a person."

"I want to kill them," he said.

"I know you do," she said. "A very large part of me wants you to do it."

"That's a horrible thing to say," Shaine said. "You have a purpose and not everyone has that in life. You should be grateful."

"What is that bird doing here?" Carleen stood and went to the window. "It's beautiful. I wonder how much someone would pay for it." She opened the window.

Mustachio flew in and perched on the chair behind Sebastian, head curled over his own. Sebastian thought of Nina and his family back on Charybdis. He thought of Alois and Fire and Death waiting for his call. He thought of his sisters safe onboard the Blue Sparrow. He closed his eyes and focused on the circuits in the collar around his neck. With a bit of fire applied, it popped off in seconds. He reached deep below and pulled, using the earth element.

"What the hell?" Qeavan's voice held pure surprise. The bastard squeaked when the house rumbled. It would be so easy to kill them all.

"What's happening?" The panic in Carleen's voice didn't bring him any pleasure. She screamed when roots burst through the floor of the kitchen and wrapped around her. It happened so quickly. One moment, they all stood around Sebastian. The next, they were wrapped in roots, from their feet to their throats.

Sebastian opened his eyes and stood. Mustachio flew out the window, returning to the ship. They would be leaving soon. He met his parents' eyes. "I'm not your son, and I'm not a scared child anymore. I will protect my family from you, don't doubt that. This is your one and only warning. If I see you again, I will kill you." He turned to Qeavan. "You aren't even worth my time. You've made enough enemies that someone will kill you soon enough."

"I'm proud of you, sweetheart," Gramma said. "I think this was the best choice for you, and I don't know if I could have made it myself. Now, if you go to my spawn's office, I'll show you where he put my will and the last of my belongings. I left them to you, but he kept them."

Sebastian ignored their screams and crying and followed his Gramma up the stairs. It didn't take long to find what Gramma wanted him to look for. He took a few minutes to pack up as many of his sisters' things as he could. He knew they had only taken what wouldn't be too suspicious. He zipped up the last bag, then turned and found Alois in the bedroom doorway.

His lip trembled for just a moment, and then he found himself wrapped in his mate's arms. "Damn, beautiful," Alois said, nuzzling his neck. They stood that way for a while, until Fire came in.

He was eating a sandwich. "Hey, Death says we should go soon. I'll help you carry stuff." He grabbed a couple of bags in his free hand.

"Where did you get the sandwich?" Alois frowned at the element, and Sebastian just grinned.

"In the kitchen," Fire said and shrugged. He left, heading downstairs.

Alois just sighed and grabbed the rest of the bags. "Anything else here they'll need?"

"Salla's art pieces," Gramma said, pointing at the closet. "If you can carry them. She really didn't want to leave them behind."

Sebastian opened the closet and pulled out the five canvases. One was huge, but the others were smaller. "We need to bring these for Salla."

Somehow, they got everything to the shuttle. Alois pulled Sebastian against his side as Death drove them back to the ship. Fire sat in the front and gnawed on the chicken leg he'd pulled out of the fridge as they left the house.

"I sent your conversation to Ava," Alois said. "She's filling out a report already and will make sure the right people get it. There shouldn't be any fallout since they confessed to what they were planning. Legally, they could sell the girls, but not you. That will be enough to get them in trouble."

"Good," Sebastian said, settling his head against Alois's chest.

"I also sent it to Fasi, Renee, Ma, and Pops." Alois

kissed the top of his head. "They're going to hug you so hard when we get back."

Sebastian smiled. He didn't mind that one bit. They drove the shuttle straight into the ship, and the ramp closed behind them. Alois helped him out of the shuttle, and he quickly found himself with an armful of Sai and Salla. His sisters were so different, he thought as he hugged them tightly. They were short, tiny little things, but damn, their arms were tight around him.

"Oh gods, they look just like you," Alois said, laughing. "Look at those eyes and those ears!"

"They're mini Sebastians," Fire said, nodding. He stood, bouncing, and waited for his hugs. Sebastian felt the ship take off, but all the crew except for Linc were here, unloading supplies and visiting with the new stowaways.

Sebastian loosened his hold on his sisters and turned them toward Alois and Fire. He couldn't make himself let them go. "This is my life-mate, Alois." His mate smiled and waved. "This is my friend, Fire." Fire jumped into the hug, and Sebastian laughed. "Also, over there in the corner is my friend, Death."

"Those are weird names," Sai said. Her brown hair was short and messy, and she was dressed in plain clothes. He hated to stereotype, but she looked just like Nina always had, like a science nerd.

"We're kinda weird people," Fire said and kissed the top of her head. His head turned sharply when a guinea pig in a large ball rolled into the cargo bay. "Fluffy, fluffy, fluffy." He let them go and took off after the ball.

The guinea pig saw him coming and turned around, rolling away.

"That was Marshmallow," Salla said. She was dressed in brightly colored clothes, and her long brown hair was twisted into an intricate pile at the top of her head. Long earrings dangled from her ears, and bracelets of all kinds jangled from her wrists. "Jellybean is around here somewhere in her ball too. They love to play chase."

"Our cat, Mocha, is sleeping on your mate's pillow," Sai said. She gave Alois an apologetic look. "I'm sorry, but she really liked it, so it belongs to her now."

Alois rolled his eyes. "Sounds like the other women in our lives."

"She tried to be friends with Linc's cat, Nugget, but she hissed at Mocha and scared her," Sai said.

"Hissy demon cat," Morgan said, growling from across the room.

Sebastian wiped the tears from his eyes. He loved his mate and their friends. Their easy acceptance made everything so much easier. "It's so good to see you two again. I'm sorry I didn't call immediately; because of that, I almost let them sell you."

"You didn't *let* them do anything," Sai said, frowning up at him. She framed his face with her small hands. "They hurt you, Sebby. We missed you so much, but we didn't blame you for not reaching out once you were free. We know you love us."

"They were the ones who didn't deserve to see you," Salla added. She wrapped her thin arms around his waist and laid her head on his chest. "What they planned is on them. You know we weren't even surprised, right? Mr. Philbert thought we would argue when he told us, but we kind of knew they were up to something."

"Oh," Sai said and pushed him away. She ran to two people standing with Dru and Morgan. She pulled a young man back over to Sebastian. "This is my life-mate, Lorry."

Sebastian raised a brow and looked at Gramma. The spirit stood talking to Death. She looked over at him and blinked innocently. Lorry wasn't exactly delicate. The boy was only fifteen, Sebastian knew that from their research. However, he was huge. The Betonize boy was just under six feet tall and had long horns atop his head. His fangs glistened when he smiled. However, Sebastian noticed the boy's clawed hand trembled in Sai's, and a blush covered the young man's cheeks.

"You're too young to have a life-mate," Alois said, scowling. His arms were crossed over his chest. Lorry's trembling increased.

"Alois, give him a break," Sebastian said and hugged the boy. "Sai and Lorry aren't getting married tomorrow. They were just really lucky and met each other early." Lorry gave him a grateful smile.

"You two better not have had sex yet," Alois said. "That needs to wait until you're both older. You know how to use protection, right?"

"Alois," Sai wailed, blushing at his words.

Salla cackled beside her sister. "Oh gods, this is great."

Alois turned to her. "Don't think I don't notice how short that skirt is, young lady." Salla growled, but Alois's eyes just narrowed.

Sai grinned and poked her sister. "This will be great, Salla. We'll need to be there for poor little Nina when she gets older. Her favorite aunts can protect her from her overprotective papa."

"If we make it that long," Salla said, sighing. "My legs are sexy and need to be properly displayed. How will I survive without short skirts?"

"You'll have to manage," Alois said. "Don't worry. We can find some Charybdis Station uniforms around here. They look great on everyone. Hazel? Do you have a spare uniform?"

Sebastian laughed as Hazel turned and ran. His sisters groaned but returned to his arms. This mission definitely had some perks.

19

PLANET VEXTONAR, SILVERLIGHT SYSTEM

Alois leaned back on one of the couches in the commons with Valentine Philbert and his small, fuzzy dog, Midge. The small Old-Earth Maltese slept on her back, legs in the air while Mocha sat on his lap, purring. The fat, chocolate-colored cat followed Alois everywhere, and he didn't know what Peri was going to think when he got home. He felt like he was cheating on his dog.

"I heard about this guy," Val said. "Air." The Betonize man was just like his son, large and gentle. Hack had already called him and talked him into working with Blue Sector's engineers when they got back home.

"After the first planet was attacked, the Lord Admiral made sure the media was aware of what he looked like and what he could do," Alois said.

"I didn't believe it," Val said. "Not until that one reporter caught some of it live." The reporter hadn't lived long, but the recording of his death had damn well convinced the galaxy that Air wasn't some myth.

"What I don't get is why he's just hanging out on Vextonar," Alois said, stroking Mocha's back.

"Waiting on someone maybe," Val said. "If he wanted to destroy the planet, it would be gone by now."

"Yeah, but what is he waiting on?"

Val looked at him nervously. "You heard about Humans First, right?"

"Yeah. We're tracking their movements," Alois said.

"They've been really clear about wanting Air on their side. It doesn't hurt that this monster looks human," Val said.

"Your man there has a good point," a voice said from behind him.

Alois yelled and jumped in his seat. Mocha wasn't pleased. He turned around and glared at Beol. "Since when did you get here?"

"Just now," Beol replied and hopped over the couch. He wiggled down in the soft cushions. "Snuck my whole ship on board. You all really need to work on your tech."

"Hay is working with our best engineers," Alois said, growling when Beol propped his feet on Alois's legs.

"Hay says this guy named Beck is pretty good." Beol looked thoughtful. "Maybe I should steal him from Fasi."

"Good luck with that," Alois said, smiling. As if anyone could steal Beck. Over half the station would fight for him.

"Back to the topic," Val said. "You think Humans First might be involved here?"

"I do," Beol said. "Right now, Air is just floating there. He has a ship full of the last of the Concords and seems to be waiting. Considering we're on Vextonar, it seems likely Humans First is who he's waiting for."

"Fuck," Alois said.

"Yeah," Val said. "That group does *not* need a weapon like Air."

"Where the hell is Beol? I just walked into his damn ship in the cargo bay." Dru yelped. "Damn it, Mustachio! Leave my hair alone."

"Mustachio?" Beol shot him a questioning look.

"My mate's bird. Don't kill him." Alois peeked over the couch. "Dru, he's in here."

"Beol! If you park your damn ship in my cargo bay, the least you can do is make it visible."

"Where's the fun in that?"

"So, anyway," Alois said, not liking the way Dru's eye was twitching. "Beol said Air is waiting for Humans First to show up. We should take care of things quickly, right?"

"Conference room," Dru said "Now." She turned on her heel and left the commons. "Fuck, Mustachio. Put Monty down!"

Alois, Beol, and Val entered the conference room. Sebastian waved at Alois from the table, and he kissed his mate before sitting beside him.

"Mustachio brought Monty to me a few minutes ago," Sebastian said and passed the little newt to Alois.

Alois put him on the table, and the newt ran

straight to Dru. She glared at them before putting the newt onto her shoulder. She turned her attention to the rest of the room. "Beol is here to update us." She gestured to the assassin and he stood.

"My team and I have been tracking Air for a while. He finally came to a stop here on Vextonar, but he refuses to shift out of his elemental form. We believe he is waiting here to make contact with Humans First."

"We need to move fast then," Morgan said.

"Yes," Beol said. "What's the plan?"

"I can freeze his form and progress time to spark a change to his human form," Death said. "However, he is damn strong and will attack immediately."

"What can he do in a battle?" Beol propped his chin on his fist. "We've seen how he can ravage a planet, but what about an actual fight?"

"He can tear you to pieces," Fire said. He jumped up and moved to sit with Sebastian. "That's what he did to that poor boy on Dargner."

"In the Crellic System? You mean Roger Belcort? He's the dead body still lying in pieces on Dargner," Beol said.

Fire nodded. "Air got mad because the Queen gave him an old body like me. She was saving the younger man for Death's body."

"Air threw a fit and tore Roger apart?" Dru looked green.

"Yeah," Fire said. "There were lots of people to choose from because of Admiral Sharp, but she stuck Air and me into older people." He patted his face. "I like my wrinkles. They make me wise." He tried for a wise face but started giggling.

Alois shook his head and smiled at Fire. "So, he can tear people apart," Alois said. "What can we do then?"

"Use my shields," Beol said. "If we can get him in his human form, we can sneak and stick him with Wyatt's poison. Then he explodes and we grab his artifact."

"Simple enough," Dru said.

"The problem is that he's surrounded by Concords. He won't leave the ship, and they're packed on it," Beol said. "They sold off all their prisoners to make more room for soldiers."

"Two teams?" Morgan pulled up schematics for the Concord ship.

"How did you get those?" Beol leaned forward.

"Dottie got them for us," Morgan said. The woman ran the spaceports on Vextonar, and Alois knew she had a soft spot for Charybdis Station. She had given them Leti and Draif. "One team goes straight to Air, and the other team works on clearing out the ship once the battle starts?"

"I thought you said Beol's shields made you invisible?" Val said, brow furrowed.

"It's more complicated than that, but yes, they do," Beol said.

"Why not try to figure a way to kill the Concords onboard first?" Val said. "It would take the surprise away from the attack on Air, but it would let everyone focus on him, right? Instead of splitting our attention?"

"Good idea," Dru said. "What can we use to kill the Concords on the ship? Death needs to be a secret weapon, so harvesting their souls is out. That would tell Air exactly who was coming."

Sebastian squeaked and covered his mouth with his hands. His eyes were wide and full of tears as he stared at the empty space next to Dru. "Beautiful? Are you seeing another spirit?"

"Yes, he is," Death said, voice cracking. Tears filled the man's eyes too. "Nina."

"She's my third spirit guide," Sebastian said. "She says Dr. Morrick knows a compound to inject in their air supply. It will kill them instantly. Then we can filter the ship and go get Air."

"Nina," Death said. His eyes were still on the spot Alois assumed the spirit stood. "I'm so sorry I couldn't save you."

Fire jumped up and ran to hug Death. "Don't cry, Death."

"Nina is yelling at him," Sebastian said, laughing wetly. "She's telling him off for feeling guilty."

"Good," Dru said. "From what he told us, he tried his best."

"Her plan is a good one," Lerais said. "Hazel and I can sneak to the ship's docking space and tamper with the air supply, then we lower their cargo bay door while the rest of you wait, ready to board."

"Val and Linc remain on board to guard the ship and the kids," Dru said, nodding. "You and Hazel get back to the ship as soon as you're done too. I think this is as good as it's going to get. Let's pass Wyatt's poison out to everyone. Anyone gets a chance to inject Air, take it."

"I'll get you all shields too," Beol said. "I'll meet you back here with my team. How long will it take to make the compound?"

"About thirty minutes," Death said.

"Will the compound have any effect on Air," Quinn asked.

"Probably not," Death said. "This is a new concept though, so I really have no idea."

"Alright," Beol said. "I'll be back in thirty minutes, and we'll see what happens." He left the room and the meeting ended.

Alois watched Sebastian and Death go to Nina's spot. He felt strangely happy that Nina was the third spirit guide. Sebastian missed her so much, and she was so damn smart. He was also sad that she wasn't at rest or peace or whatever came after death. Alois got up, ready to go check on the girls when he noticed Morgan. His friend stared down at the table, and his shoulders drooped.

"What's wrong?" Alois kept his voice low.

"Remember the mission to find and kill Water?"

"I do," Alois said. He was on Dru's team for that mission, but he knew what Morgan had gone through.

"Imagine if we had Beol's shields then," Morgan said. He looked up, his eyes filled with pure agony. "Our friends would still be alive."

Alois hugged Morgan, pressing the man's face into his shoulder. "We didn't have the shields then. We can't play *what if*, Morgan. There are plenty of things we could do differently with what we've learned and what we can do now. We can't change them though."

"I just… I just don't want to lose anyone again."

"Me neither," Alois said. "Our plan is pretty good though. It gives us a chance we didn't have with Water."

"We have Death now," Morgan said, sitting up and wiping his eyes. "We have Sebastian and Fire too." Alois's mate moved across the room, coming to stand next to them.

"Don't forget Mustachio," Sebastian said softly and kissed Morgan's cheek. "We can do this, Morgan. I know it."

20

Sebastian hugged Sai and Salla. He spoke softly. "If we don't come back, Val and Linc will take you all to Charybdis Station. Stay with Nina, okay? Make sure she grows up happy."

"We will, Sebby," Salla said, voice thick with tears. "We'll do right by her."

"We won't need to though," Sai said. She shook him a bit. "You'll all come back alright. We've only just found you again, Sebby. Plus, Mocha is in love with your mate, so you all really do need to come back."

Sebastian laughed roughly. "We'll come back for Mocha. I want you guys to meet Periwinkle and her puppies too."

"That's all the reasons to live we need," Alois said from behind him. He pulled Sebastian, Sai, and Salla into a squashed hug. "We'll be good." He let them go. "Where's Lorry? I should hug the fucker too and remind him not to get romantic while I'm gone."

"Alois," Sai said, groaning.

Alois laughed as he jogged across the room to Lorry.

"Sorry, Sai," Sebastian said. "My mate is a protective daddy."

"Yeah, yeah," she said. "Just come back."

Sebastian and Alois said goodbye one more time, then joined the others at the door. Fire scooted close to Sebastian and grabbed his hand. The element wasn't trembling, but it was a close thing. He knew this had to be hard for him. Beol passed out the shields. His three fellow assassins stood behind him, faces grim.

"Activate them now, and we'll leave the ship," Dru said. "Dottie did her best to reduce traffic between the Blue Sparrow and the Concord ship, but don't bump into anyone if you can help it. We'll wait at the pre-planned spot until I get the word from Lerais."

Sebastian squeezed Fire's hand and activated his shield. One by one, they each disappeared, but Sebastian kept hold of Fire. Together, they made their way across the spaceport to the Concord ship. Sebastian saw the restroom sign Dru had mentioned and stopped. Someone from their team bumped into him from behind.

"Sorry, beautiful," Alois whispered.

Sebastian reached back and patted his mate's stomach.

They waited for about ten minutes, until Sebastian couldn't stand it. The stillness and the isolation sucked. "Okay," Dru said softly. "Lerais says they had to take out a few guards, but the air is filtered and clear. Let's do this."

They hurried to the Concord ship just in time to see the door drop down. Sebastian noticed the three bodies beside the ship. They were still breathing, so it looked like Charybdis would get a few prisoners today.

Everyone had a copy of the schematics of the ship, but Sebastian had done his best to memorize it. Beol had said Air was always on the bridge, so they ignored the dead bodies lining the hall and rushed that way.

"Something isn't right," Death said. "I can't find Air. I've always been able to sense him."

Sebastian focused and entered the spirit world as they ran. His skills as a shaman were his best weapon. As soon as the threads were visible around him, he realized his mistake. Angry silvery white and sickly green threads circled above their heads. He yelped and fell out of the spirit world. A gust of wind picked him up and pulled him down the hall. A grasping, airy hand pulled his shield off, tossing it to the ground, and seconds later, he was dropped into a room.

"Sebastian!" He heard Alois's voice cut off as the door slammed shut.

"Got you, baby shaman. My Queen gave me a fun little trick to find you when you entered the spirit world. She gave me a lot of fun tricks. *I'm* her favorite now." He heard Air's voice in his head, but the room was empty. "She wants you, baby shaman. It's been such a long time since she tortured another shaman." Sebastian was picked up again and spun around. Panic filled him, and he couldn't concentrate as Air laughed in his head. "You just walked right onto my ship. How lucky am I?"

The wall of the room exploded inward, leaving a big, melted hole, and a piece of metal debris hit his arm, cutting it deeply. Air dropped him, and he fell, hard, landing on his ankle. Sebastian felt something snap. He whimpered as he tried to stand.

"No! You stay there," Air said, and he was pushed against the wall. A circling tornado of fire came through the hole, and Sebastian felt his heart sink. Fire.

Mustachio flew above the flames and began his song. Sebastian closed his eyes and slipped into the spirit world. He couldn't let Fire get hurt. He could see them now. Fire twisted around Air's elemental form, and they mixed together, fighting for dominance. Air was determined to reach Sebastian, and Fire held him back.

"Death, freeze him," Beol said. Waves of air buffeted the others around the room. Sebastian could see Alois's threads trying to get to him, even if he couldn't see his body. The others struggled to reach Air.

"I can't. Something isn't right," Death said. "Fire and Air are too entwined, so I'd freeze them both. Their forms mixed together are too chaotic."

"What other choice do we have?" Dru's voice was full of pain, and Sebastian saw blood mix with the air. The debris had to be doing damage.

Sebastian focused on their mixed threads. He *knew* Fire. He could easily pick his innocent, joyful threads out from Air's ugliness and cruelty. He didn't know how to pull them apart though. He tried to snap one of Air's threads, but it was like steel. Mustachio sang his song and landed clumsily beside him. The air pushed them hard against the wall. Sebastian pulled him close, holding the bird in his arms.

"Alright," Death said, and the two forms froze. Death pushed time forward, and the two elements dropped to the ground, forced to change.

Fire fell to his knees. Air's white eyes were full of hate and focused on Sebastian. Torrents of air still buffeted the team around the room, even after Death froze Air again.

"Stop, damn you," Death said, frustrated.

The element fought him and managed a small hand wiggle. Small silver and white balls of air zipped around the room, and one headed toward Sebastian, impossibly fast.

"Sebastian," Fire yelled, voice full of tears. He jumped in front of Sebastian just as the ball of air reached him. Fire took the hit to his chest, and his body seemed to soak it in. Immediately, he broke into bloody pieces, limbs ripped apart.

"Fire," Sebastian cried, closing his eyes as blood splattered him. "No, no, no." He heard Morgan yell and saw a black clad lower leg fall to the ground. A hand fell from across the room, and Sebastian saw the back of it was covered in red scales. "Alois," he whimpered. The remaining six balls zipped around the room, searching for targets.

"Sebby," Nina said, crouching down beside him. "What's the opposite of air? You read those books, right?"

"You know how to end this," Tell said, standing on his other side.

"Fuck him up, sweetheart," Gramma said, standing above Nina. "That bastard wants to take you out with him."

Time seemed to stand still as Sebastian spread his awareness out, searching for earth, the opposite of air. His awareness pointed out something close to him, something unexpected. His hand covered the little seed inside him and he moved on. Vextonar was built so high from the ground, and the spaceport was at the very top. The planet wanted to help though. Life waited below, wanting to grow. Soil curled on the surface of the planet, waiting for his direction. He called it to him, and the spaceport shook. He gentled it and slowed down. No need to hurt people with an earthquake. The ship rocked and more holes appeared in the walls of the room.

"Sebastian?" Death's voice was strained, and Sebastian knew he struggled to hold Air. "He's stronger than he should be."

Sebastian's eyes opened when dirt poured in through the holes, and he fell into Mustachio's song – earth, fire, and life. He focused, and the dirt swirled into six long coils, hissing as they took the form of snakes. Fire flowed through them, hardening the dirt. His snakes zeroed in on the remaining balls, flying easily through the ear. One by one, they each swallowed a ball and curled up as it activated. His snakes' bodies shook, but held. Sebastian used the wall and stood, Mustachio in his arms.

His snakes looked at him, waiting, so he pointed at Air. They hissed and flew toward the frozen element.

They covered Air's threads, curling around him. More and more dirt poured into the ship, and Sebastian shaped them all. Each new snake wrapped around Air until his threads were covered and muffled, the silver and ugly green disappearing beneath brown and black soil. They were soon so covered, Air couldn't focus, and the torrents faded, dropping Sebastian's team to the ground.

"Free me, brother," Air said, eyes imploring Death to save him. "Our Queen wants you beside her. Take Life's place, just as you were always meant to."

Death snorted as Quinn and one of Beol's people stabbed Air with injectors at the same time. Sebastian asked his snakes to solidify around Air as the element shrieked. Wyatt's poison wasn't painless, and Sebastian couldn't make himself mind Air's suffering. Then the element was gone, exploding into bits and pieces. Sebastian winced as he heard things splattering against his snake wall.

Nina let out a breath of relief. "You all really didn't want to be contaminated with his blood and tissue. Good call, cousin."

"Dirt was a good choice, Sebastian," Death said, falling to his knees. "That could have gone very wrong. Fire?"

"He's gone," Sebastian whispered, hugging Mustachio. "Alois?"

"I'm here, beautiful." Alois's arms were around him. His mate clicked his shield button and quickly appeared. "Sebastian," he said, shaking.

"Your hand?"

Alois brought his left arm around. His hand was gone, and the stump oozed blood, even though it was wrapped. "Wrapped it while rolling around in the air," Alois said, pale. "We need Rune."

"Called him," Dru said, deactivating her shield. Monty clung to her head, and she held her shoulder looking around. "Morgan?"

"My leg got skewered," the man said, voice full of pain. "It's just debris though. Beol's buddy got hit by one of those balls."

One by one, the team deactivated their shields. One of Beol's assassins was in bad shape. Her lower right leg was gone, and blood poured out.

"Rune's on his way," Dru said. "What happened? How did Air find you, Sebastian?"

"Air said the Queen knew about me and wanted him to get me so she could *play* with me," Sebastian said. "How did she know about me?" He shook in Alois arms, eyes on what was left of Fire.

"After freeing Fire, you've become something of a Charybdis legend," Beol said from next to his fallen friend. He stood and approached the earthen wall and poked at it. "He didn't even notice Fire and Death. How did he know you were here?"

"He said the Queen taught him how to sense me when I enter the spirit world," Sebastian said, shivering. He rubbed his face against Alois. "He said she gave him a lot of tricks to use. That's why Death struggled with him. Was anyone else hurt?" Death sat beside him, back sliding down the wall. Sebastian took his hand, and they stared at Fire's remains together.

"Fucking debris," Dru said. "Quinn got hit in the stomach and another Half-Moon assassin has debris in her arm. We really need to get your names before we go into battle, damn it."

"I may have a concussion," Beol added. Sebastian noticed the knot on the man's head. "I have all my limbs though." He went back to his friend.

Rune skidded into the room, bag in hand. "Who's hurt the worst?" He followed the pointing fingers to the assassin missing the leg and got to work.

"Sebastian," Tell said. Sebastian looked up at his mentor, numb inside. "I was there when the Queen first summoned Fire into a body. I know the ritual to bring him back."

He pushed Alois into Death's arms. "Make sure my honey bear gets treated, okay? He's my mate, and I love him so damn much."

"I'll take care of him," Death said, frowning. "What are you doing?"

"Sebastian?" Alois sounded out of it.

Sebastian ignored them and stood, wincing when he realized his ankle was probably broken. "I thought the elements' essences needed to recharge or something before they could be brought back," he said to Tell.

"A rejuvenating treatment before the ritual should work," Tell said. "You need a living host though. We used volunteers, men that knew they would die, but wanted to save our world."

"Sebastian? What are you going to do?" Death's voice was full of hope.

"Tell and I have a plan, but I need help walking." Alois struggled to stand, so Sebastian leaned down and kissed his mate. "You need to stay here and get patched up, so don't even think of trying to stand."

"I can walk," Beol said.

"As can I," the only uninjured assassin said. "My name is Noe." The man reached him and picked him up. "Where do we go?"

"Beol, can you get Fire's artifact?" Sebastian asked.

Beol reached down and picked up the bloody pyramid-shaped artifact. "Got it."

"To the front of the ship," Sebastian said. He looked over Noe's shoulder. "Love you, Alois."

"Love you too, beautiful. Bring our friend back if you can, but don't risk yourself," Alois said.

"I picked out the best candidate," Tell said, following them out the door and through the halls. "The man has a nasty soul. The other two are idiots, but salvageable."

"Thanks, Tell," Sebastian said. "I never thought I'd *want* to do this."

"Are you talking to a spirit?" Beol jogged alongside them. "Wolfe told me about that."

"Tell is my mentor. He'll help me do the ritual to bring Fire back," Sebastian said. "Put me down here, please." The three unconscious men still lay beside the ship.

Tell pointed to a light-haired man. "This one." The man was barely twenty and dressed well for a mercenary.

"This guy? He's just a kid," Sebastian said.

"Trust me," Tell said. "His soul doesn't match his youthful appearance."

"At least he's a lot younger than Fire's previous body," Sebastian said. "Please get that man and put him over here." Sebastian leaned on the ship. "We need something to represent each element."

Soon enough, they had the Concord mercenary laid flat on the ground and surrounded by representations of the elements. Noe helped him hobble to each element and give it intention. Afterwards, he managed to sit beside the body. *I'll crawl if I have to move,* he thought. He placed the artifact on the man's chest. "How do we rejuvenate his essence?" Sebastian looked at Tell.

"Lay your hand on the artifact and use the life element," Tell said. "Repeat after me."

Sebastian closed his eyes and did as he was told. He spoke the long and complicated Ancient Crellic phrases. Green and gold light swirled around him and into the artifact. He could almost feel Fire dancing inside. He opened his eyes. "Done."

"Now for the ritual," Tell said. "It will take a lot of energy from you, but I will stop you before it hurts your sprout."

Sebastian patted his abdomen. The birthing line must be hidden by his tattoos. He hadn't noticed a thing before sensing it earlier. "Thanks. Let's do this."

Sebastian crawled slowly to each element and spoke the required phrases. He pushed his energy into each one, saving the fire element for last. Beol's dagger lit up with fiery heat, and Sebastian thought Dru may steal this one too since she loved the blade Beol had given her. He placed his hand on the hilt and spoke the final words, pouring everything he had into the dagger.

It flew from his hands and embedded itself in the tip of the artifact. Lines of fire raced down the artifact and into the Concord merc's body. Sebastian saw the cruelty in the man's soul and knew Tell had been right. The grey wisp left the man's body, and Sebastian pushed the last of his energy into the artifact. A bright, colorful wisp rose up from the element and floated down into the body. "He has a soul," Sebastian said in surprise. "Fire has a soul."

"That's enough energy, Sebastian," Tell said, and Sebastian let go. He lay on the ground and watched Fire sit up. Sebastian closed his eyes and let sleep take him, smiling when he heard Fire.

"Sebby!"

21

SILVERLIGHT SYSTEM, EN ROUTE TO CHARYBDIS STATION

Alois watched Sebastian sleep in their bed. Fire and his new body were curled up on one side of Sebastian and Alois claimed the other. When he had seen Noe come back in carrying an unconscious Sebastian, he thought he'd go insane. Fire watched him, face worried, while Death sat at the end of the bed, eyes on Sebastian's face. The man had stayed with Alois and made sure Rune looked over his stumb and treated his other wounds.

"He's fine, guys," Rune said. "He's just exhausted. I set his ankle and covered it in cast seal. His arm had a nasty cut, but I fixed it. Otherwise, he's just fine." Rune looked over his shoulder at Sai and Salla. The girls sat on the couch together, both curled up with Lorry. They had been so upset. Alois had almost laughed when the poor guy ended up with both sisters in his lap. He couldn't comfort one and not the other. The kid would make a good addition to their family. Eventually.

"There is one thing," Rune said with a grin.

"Is Sebby going to die?" Fire looked miserable.

"No, Fire," Rune said softly. "He'll be fine. When I was running tests on him, I did find out Alois and Sebastian are going to be daddies again. Nina will have a little brother or sister in about eight months."

Alois felt his eyes water. He looked down at Sebastian. His mate was pale with dark shadows under his eyes. His poor ankle and shoulder were bandaged. Alois looked at his mate's belly. Sebastian had been so happy that he finally lost most of the baby weight from carrying Nina. He grinned and covered Sebastian's abdomen with his remaining hand. His baby was in there. He'd get to see Sebastian grow with his child. He'd be there this time.

Fire sat up and pressed his ear against Sebastian's abdomen. "Baby, can you hear me?"

Sai and Salla scooted onto the bed, doing their best not to jostle Sebastian or Alois. "We'll be the best aunts in the galaxy," Salla said. "We'll make sure Nina doesn't feel left out either."

"Okay," Rune said. "Alois and Sebastian both need a lot of rest. Let them sleep and give them lots of food when they wake up."

"We will," Sai said. She got back up and pulled Salla and Fire off the bed. "Come on. Let's go check on the others. We can see if they need any help and let them all know that Sebastian is fine. Beol left his ship in the cargo bay. They're going to ride home with us."

"I need to chase Jellybean and Marshmallow," Fire said. "I didn't get my daily chasing in this morning."

"You know what? This new body of yours matches

you a lot better," Salla said. They headed for the door. "An old guy running around the ship was just weird."

"Any adult running around the ship chasing guinea pigs is weird," Sai said. She held Lorry's hand as they all left the room.

"I'll leave too," Death said. "I wanted to thank Sebastian for all he did. It's never been that hard to hold Air before. I didn't even think about the Queen doing something to him."

"You two worked well together," Alois said. "You know he'd do it all again in a heartbeat, Morrick. He loves Fire."

"He does," Death said, grinning. "I couldn't have wished for better keepers for Fire."

"Keepers? Now wait a second," Alois said. Death was out the door almost before he finished speaking. Alois sighed.

Rune chuckled as he loaded his bag back up. "You two need to add on to your house."

Alois groaned and lay back down. "We do." He peeked up at Rune. "When are you and Silas getting a place of your own?"

Rune blushed. "We've talked about it, but Leti still needs guarding."

"You know I have an empty house just sitting down the road, right?"

"We'll save up, and maybe we can buy it from you," Rune said, smiling.

"Rune, don't be an idiot. My house is yours when you're ready for it." Alois smiled at the man's shocked face. "You saved my life so many damn times back on

Tammol. You're my crewmate and my friend. Plus, you and Silas are too damn adorable together. Do you have any idea how many pictures of the two of you I've sent to everyone?"

"Alois," Rune said. "I'll talk to you again when you're not hopped up on pain meds." He shook his head, smiling, and headed for the door.

"Answer won't change, Rune," Alois said. He settled against Sebastian. Mustachio sang from his perch in the corner, a low and sweet lullaby. He fell asleep, imagining Nina playing with a little girl or boy.

———

"THEN, Sebby brought me back in my new body," Fire said. He put his hands to his face. "I miss my wrinkles. I was so wise." They all sat in front of the vid-screen, spending some time with their three favorite couples – Renee and Fasi, Ma and Pops, and Leti and Hack."

Renee and Fasi shared a look while the others laughed. "Your new body looks good, Fire," Renee said, laughing. "We can't wait for you all to get home."

"Pops and I talked," Fasi said. "We decided to go ahead and start an addition to your house."

"Sebastian needs his own office, and you two could use a couple more rooms to grow your family," Pops said.

"Fasi," Sebastian said. "That's too much money to spend without telling us."

"I'm your dad, Sebastian," Fasi said smugly. "I have

video of you saying so. This is what dads do. They take care of their children."

"Listen to your father, Sebastian," Pops said. "Both of us."

"You two are ridiculous," Sebastian said, throwing his hands in the air.

"Anyway," Leti said, giggling. "We registered Sai and Salla for school too. You two will love Charybdis Station's school. At least that's what Rose says."

"I talked to her yesterday," Sai said. "She checked and the science program is top notch." She nodded. "I'll be fine."

"Good for you, but Charybdis Station doesn't even have an art program," Salla said. "What am I going to do?"

"We've started one for you, sweetie," Ma said. "I talked to some of the other mothers and the principal. With so many new families on Charybdis, we need to branch out."

"Seriously?" Salla smiled widely. "You did that for me?"

"I'm Sebastian's mother," Ma said. "He said so. We have video." She winked at Sebastian as he sputtered. "That means you and Sai are mine. Lorry and his papa are ours too; they just don't know it yet."

"I'm so happy our parents tried to sell us," Salla said.

Alois snorted. "Best thing ever, right?"

"Is Selene still alright taking care of Nina?" Sebastian rolled his eyes at them, then looked back at the screen. "A baby is a lot of work."

"We just talked to them fifteen minutes ago," Sai

said. Sebastian glared at his sister, and Alois kissed his mate's cheek. They both missed Nina.

"She's fine, of course," Fasi said. "I swear that woman could do anything and do it better than all of us put together."

"She is amazing," Sebastian said, sighing. He shook his head and moved on. "Leti, how are Shae and Juniper doing?"

"Good," Leti said. "Juniper hired more people for the diner so he could help Astus in the gardens more often. Shae is dating a pilot named Liam Doney." Leti growled, sounding like a fierce baby.

"Aww, that's so cute," Sai said.

"I'm not cute," Leti said. "I'm tough, and I don't like this Doney guy."

"He does have a reputation," Alois said. Shae was entirely capable of taking care of himself, but he was Selene's little brother. That meant he was all of Blue Solace's little brother.

"You two will let Shae have a life," Renee said. "He deserves to have a little fun."

"Alois, do you want to spy on him when you get home?" Leti asked.

"Oh yeah," Alois said. "We can use Beol's shields. No one will see us."

"That is *not* how I wanted to integrate Half-Moon's technology," Fasi said, grumbling. "I'll come along too. Just to make sure you two behave."

Renee threw her hands in the air. "Sai, Salla, I apologize in advance for these idiots."

"He made me throw out all my short skirts," Salla said, glaring at Alois.

"We'll get you some new ones, dearie," Ma said. "A girl deserves to feel pretty."

"They were way too short," Alois said indignantly. They didn't understand.

"He may have a point, darling," Pops said. Ma glared at him and he hushed up. Alois didn't blame him. Ma didn't cook for anyone if they made her mad.

"Moving on," Salla said. "How are the puppies?"

Damn little sister knew what would distract him, Alois thought, scowling.

Hack sat up and grinned. "My grandpuppies are the cutest little fluffballs in the galaxy."

"I can't wait to hold them," Alois said, arms feeling empty. He grabbed Fire and squeezed him in a hug. The element giggled. "Have we found good homes for them?"

"Haroon is getting one," Sebastian said.

"He didn't really agree," Hack said.

"Too bad," Leti said. "He needs a puppy."

"Okay," Alois said slowly. "One to Haroon. What about giving one to Silas and Rune? I'm giving them my house."

Leti clapped happily. "Yes! They are so cute together."

"I like that idea," Hack said. "Silas can still spend the day guarding Leti without having to live there." He scowled. "Wolfe moved in and decided he's Leti's new guard anyway."

"I love having Wolfe close by," Leti said. "Beol doesn't like it, but that butthead can deal."

"I can't believe you don't like someone," Sebastian said. "Beol seems like just the type of person you would grab hold of and make be your friend."

"Don't let him fool you," Hack said. "I found him in his office plotting ways to make Beol like him. He had a chart and everything."

Alois laughed as Leti blushed.

"Oh, I see," Sebastian said. "He acts like he doesn't like you, so you act like you don't like him."

"He just hasn't met me yet," Leti said.

"Leti," Fire said. "I heard Beol tell his friend Ninnetta that you will probably try to make her stay with you because her leg is gone. He said you will go all mama hen on her." Fire set his head on Alois's shoulder. "Beol likes you just fine. He's just shy."

"Beol's shy?" Leti looked thoughtful.

"Plotting," Hack said. "See? I told you."

Sai cleared her throat. "So, one more puppy."

"Beck," Alois said suddenly. "He needs a puppy to love."

"His feet are still itchy," Ma said. "A puppy might hold him over until he meets his mate."

"There you go," Leti said. "Puppies are all accounted for. We can neuter Gravy and spay Peri after the puppies are weaned."

"Hold on," Hack said.

Alois nodded furiously. "We need to think about it a little more. Those puppies are damn cute, and Peri and Gravy love each other."

"Oh, you're okay with them being together now?" Sebastian's brow raised.

"I've had time to process," Alois said. "Peri is a good dog parent, and Gravy is a really good catch."

"Sai, Salla," Renee said. "Again, I apologize for these idiots."

22

CHARYBDIS STATION, ANCHOR'S REST
SYSTEM

"We're home," Fire yelled, running down the ship's ramp. He went straight to Ma. "I missed your waffles, Ma." Mustachio flew out of the ship, soaring above them, already headed home.

Sebastian ignored him and went straight to Selene and Haroon. "Nina," he said and took his girl. She had grown in the time they were gone. He couldn't believe she was almost a year old.

"Dada," she said and snuggled into him.

"Alois! Alois! Nina said dada," Sebastian cried, squealing and bouncing. He spun around, looking for his mate.

Alois was right behind him, grinning widely. "I heard her. She's the smartest baby in the whole galaxy."

"New parents," Selene said, shaking her head.

"She is a smart girl," Haroon argued.

Sebastian blew her a kiss and laughed hard when Leti wrapped his arms around him from behind. "Sebastian, you're finally home."

"He kind of missed you," Hack said, smiling. He hugged Alois. "We all did."

"Nina said dada," Sebastian told his friend. "She's so smart."

"Aww," Leti crooned. "She's the sweetest little girl ever. Pepper is the smartest, but you're a close second, Nina." He tickled her belly.

"Hmm," Haroon said. "I foresee baby contests in the future."

"Where is your brood?" Alois looked around for Leti's army.

"Shae and Juniper are working on the food for our welcome home party," Leti said. "I left the kids with Grandpa Moses. He put most of them to work."

"Good man," Alois said, nodding.

Sebastian settled into Alois's side and looked around. Quinn and Cordelia were in each other's arms, Biscuit trapped between them. Morgan and Death were caught up in a family hug with Wyatt, Estella, and the twins. Rune and Silas were holding hands, heads pressed together, and eyes closed. Sebastian nodded to Alois, and his mate took a picture of the two men. So cute!

Pops had an arm wrapped around Val's shoulders, and the two men were already talking about Val's new job in engineering. Beck stood with them, holding a wiggling puppy in his arms. It was a black and grey fluffball with little horns. Renee and Fasi were in the middle of hugging Sai, Salla, and Lorry. Almost all of Half-Moon had shown up to greet their people. They joined in with the rest of the crew and grabbed bags, starting to unload the ship. Beol walked down the ramp, carrying Jellybean and Marshmallow in their balls, and Sebastian was so damn happy he was watching him.

The man paused mid-step, eyes going wide. He shook his head and scanned the docks. He looked horrified, maybe even afraid. "Guild Master?" Noe said, stopping beside him. "Are you alright? Moyra is helping Ninnetta. What's wrong?"

Wolfe ran up the ramp, eyes trained on his brother. He looked around the docks, searching for whatever had Beol's attention. Beol ignored his friend and grabbed his brother in a hug, eyes looking from face to face in the crowd gathered. Sebastian followed his gaze, looking around their friends. He gasped and covered his mouth when he saw Beck. The large green Grell stared at Beol, eyes wide and adoring. He clutched his tail in one hand and a puppy in the other.

"Alois, I think Beck and Beol are life-mates," Sebastian said.

"What?" Alois looked at Beck, then started grinning.

Leti gasped. "That's perfect. Absolutely perfect."

"No," Hack said. "Beck needs a gentle and sweet mate."

"What are Beol's qualifications?" Selene tilted her head, staring at the assassin. "I don't like this."

Beck smiled shyly at Beol and waved, forgetting his tail was in his hand. Sebastian's eyes flew to Beol. The assassin's face cleared and softened. His smile was clearly rusty and a bit strained, but it was there. He waved back.

"Boss?" Noe started grinning. He looked at Wolfe. "Is it really happening?"

Wolfe nodded energetically, grinning.

"Yes." Noe pumped his fist in the air. "I'm telling everyone." He spun around and started heading toward the other Half-Moon assassins.

Wolfe looked over at Sebastian and Leti and winked. Then he headed to the nearest assassin.

"No," Hack said. "Not happening."

"I don't like it," Selene repeated.

Sebastian leaned up and kissed Alois. "It's so happening," he whispered to his mate.

SEBASTIAN LEANED BACK in his chair, stuffed. "Oh gods, I can't eat anymore." Mustachio swooped up and down, trilling happily above them.

"I'll clean your plate," Fire said and grabbed Sebastian's mostly empty plate. "Ma and Juniper are my favorite people." He paused, giving Sebastian a dismayed look. "After you, Death, and Nina. That's what I meant to say."

"I know you love me, sweetie," Sebastian said, patting his hand.

Alois yawned and laid his head in Sebastian's lap. He sat on the ground in front of Sebastian's chair. "It's so good to be home."

"It is," Sebastian said. He ran his fingers through Alois's brown, silky hair. Nina slept in Alois's lap, tuckered out from all the excitement of the day.

Sebastian thought he might join her soon. Periwinkle and Mocha curled up together against Alois's side. The two had decided to share Alois. "Oh, look at Saia and Salla." His sisters and Rose were huddled together, laughing.

"Where's Lorry? I hope he's not feeling left out," Alois said.

Sebastian laughed. "I thought you didn't want him near Sai for another five years."

"I don't," Alois said defensively. "He just doesn't really know anyone else here. Oh, there he is." He nodded toward the table of food. Lorry, Mo, and Alex stood together, arms crossed, looking tough. "I think they're guarding the food from Trixie."

The goat stood behind the boys, chewing on the tablecloth. "Yeah, they're failing," Sebastian said. "I think Grandpa Moses is going to help. Oh. Nope. He got distracted by the littles." Sami, Rizzie, Xu, and Dannol's little girl, Nessa, intercepted the older Burnished man. They wanted to play, and Grandpa Moses was happy to help.

"Can Siren men have babies?" Sebastian asked. His eyes were on Shae. The young Siren sat surrounded by babies. Wyatt and Morgan's twins were on one side, while Pepper, Sofie, and Milo were on the other. He seemed perfectly content.

"I don't know," Alois said. "I don't think so, but there aren't really a lot of Sirens on Charybdis Station."

"He's going to need a baby of his own one day," Sebastian said, nodding toward Shae.

"Oh, cousin," Nina's spirit said. "You're going to love

watching his mating." She sat in the grass, leaning back on her hands.

"Don't be telling things you shouldn't, Nina," Gramma said, perching on a pile of pillows.

"I didn't," Nina said defensively.

Sebastian ignored them and looked around for Tell. The large Crellic shaman was in the corner, talking to Death. Wyatt and Morgan watched the one-sided conversation with interest. Fasi and Renee grabbed his attention when they sat in the chairs beside them.

"How are you feeling, Sebastian? Any morning sickness?" Fasi's purple face was full of concern.

"Thank the gods, no," Sebastian said. "I'm just a month and a half along, but so far, so good."

"What about your hand, Alois?" Renee gave him a sympathetic look. "You'll have a robotic one fitted soon."

"I'm okay," Alois said. "It could have been so much worse."

Sebastian thought of Fire's body exploding. Yeah, it really could have.

"We haven't made it common knowledge yet," Renee said. "Wyatt and Leti are ready to permanently destroy Life, Air, and Water."

"We're going to do it tonight," Fasi said. "We'll let the media know afterwards."

"Any more theft attempts?" Sebastian asked.

"Seventeen since you all left," Renee said. "All working for Humans First."

"The Concords are gone now, but Humans First is becoming a problem," Fasi said.

"At least they don't have the elements on their side," Alois said. "The Queen is Silet. Surely, they won't even consider working with her."

"I… don't know," Renee said. "She usually stays on her home world, but a connection to Humans First isn't impossible."

"We'll have a problem taking her out," Sebastian said. He winced. "She's a shaman, so she can see in the spirit world. Beol's shields won't do us a damn bit of good."

"She stays in the spirit world," Fire said, shuddering. "It's spooky."

"Fuck," Fasi said, then shook his head. "That's a problem for another day. Let's enjoy the food and our family."

"We're relieved you all are back and safe," Renee said. She hugged Sebastian, then crouched down to hug Alois. "You boys are our family and we love you." Fasi and Renee moved on to Dru and Lerais, and Sebastian tried not to cry.

"I love this place," he said.

"Me too, beautiful," Alois said.

"Me three," Fire said, then burped. "I need more food." He jumped up and ran to the table, pushing between Alex and Lorry. "Here, Trixie. Try some cake."

"I love that doofus too," Sebastian said.

"He's our son, isn't he?"

"Yes." Sebastian nodded firmly.

"Look at all the Half-Moon assassins," Alois said. "They look like timid kids at a school dance."

He was right, Sebastian thought. The Charybdis

bunch ran around, playing, laughing, and eating. The Half-Moon assassins sat together, watching everything and everyone, especially Beck and Beol. Sebastian couldn't really blame them. The Grell kept bringing food and drinks and flowers to Beol. Beck would give the assassin his gift, then sit beside him a minute before he got nervous and ran back to his friends. Then, he'd get something else, and it would all start over.

"That's going to be fun to watch," Sebastian said, stroking Alois's hair. Love and life-mates were funny things.

EPILOGUE

*A*lois and Sebastian sat on the couch watching the final season of Love's Perfect Match. The show was canceled now in the wake of the destruction of Elusa. Sebastian snuggled into his mate, happy for the privacy. Nina was sleeping in her nursery, Mustachio and Periwinkle on guard duty. Sai and Salla were settled down for the night in their own newly constructed bedrooms, and Fire was asleep in his room. How long he would stay there, Sebastian didn't know.

"I can't believe we're getting married in two weeks," Sebastian said. "Ava has everything ready and it's going to be perfect."

"I can't wait to see Hack's wedding hat," Alois said, snickering. "Oh, Beck came by this morning for advice. He's going to ask Beol to be his date for the wedding."

"Aww," Sebastian said.

We interrupt this program for an important announcement. The show disappeared, and a news reporter appeared on the vid-screen. *What you're about to see is very graphic and not appropriate for young children.* The picture shifted to a familiar neighborhood.

"Is that my parents' house?" Sebastian swallowed hard.

Earlier today, a bystander recorded this footage. A Silet woman landed on Union Station at 5:15 in the morning. At 7:13, she arrived at a suburban neighborhood. The news reporter's face twisted in horror, and the screen switched to the recording.

"That's the Queen," Sebastian said.

The Queen stood outside his parents' house and smiled. She held her arms out and began to speak, Ancient Crellic pouring from her mouth. The earth around her began to rise, and the ground started to split. His parents' house disappeared into the ground, and soon, every house in the neighborhood followed. The video went black, and the news reporter's face reappeared.

This woman somehow managed to cause Union Station to experience multiple earthquakes. At this time, video shows most of the surface of the planet is rubble. At 9:00 tonight, our Station received a message from Humans First. They said the following: Humans are not meant to be second-class citizens in this galaxy. They are meant to rule the lesser species. Union Station was a planet full of non-humans. With the help of our ally, the Queen, we have purified it.

"Alois, is this real?" Sebastian hid his face against his mate.

"Fuck," Alois said. His comm started chiming. "The Queen has made her move."

The Blue Solace Series – science fiction/fantasy, mpreg

1. The Mercenary's Mate – https://amzn.to/2MAOFEH
2. The General's Mate – https://amzn.to/2G1abRE
3. The Soldier's Mate – https://amzn.to/2S7R6ng
4. The Lieutenant's Mate – https://amzn.to/2THZ47w
5. The Engineer's Mate – https://amzn.to/2HpI4vH
6. The Captain's Mate – https://amzn.to/2knP03W
7. The Rebel's Mate – *Coming Soon*
8. Fire's Mate – *Coming Soon*

The Hobson Hills Omegas – non-shifter, mpreg, omegaverse

1. Falling for the Omega – https://amzn.to/2BgWURV
2. Snow Kisses for My Omega – https://amzn.to/2TdDiol
3. Romancing the Omega – https://amzn.to/2UNENKD

4. Healing the Omega – https://amzn.to/2FNcXrY
5. A Pint for my Omega – https://amzn.to/2XItQf7
6. Unraveling the Omega – https://amzn.to/2xRCnRL
7. The Alpha's Christmas Wish – https://amzn.to/2rsfGnF
8. Noah's story (Title to be determined) – *Coming Soon*

Hobson Hills Shorts – short stories from the world of Hobson Hills Omegas

1. The Beta's Love Song – https://amzn.to/2UrRPNN
2. Bennett's Dream – https://amzn.to/2GwSpG3
3. Justin's Journey – https://amzn.to/2DhW1t1
4. Grey's Gift – https://amzn.to/2BcjxXf
5. Hobson Hills Shorts: Volume One – https://amzn.to/2M3oGGZ

Holiday Omegas Shorts – holiday short stories from the world of The Silver Isles – paranormal, mpreg

1. Cauldron Cake Pops and a Witch's Kiss – https://amzn.to/33wMrhc
2. Sugar Cookies and a Witch's Love – *Coming December, 2019*
3. Candy Hearts and a Witch's Ring – *Coming in*

February, 2020

The Silver Isles – paranormal, mermen, mpreg

1. The Guppy Prince – https://amzn.to/2q9Q8en
2. The Not so Little Merman – *Coming Soon*
3. The Sea Witch – *Coming Soon*

If you would like to keep up with releases, please like and follow me on Instagram (@c.w._gray) or Facebook (@cwgrayauthor), join C.W. Gray's Reading Nook on Facebook, or visit my website at https://cwgray-author.com.

Excerpt from *The Engineer's Mate*, book five in The Blue Solace

"Beckie Boo, you can't mean that." Ma's sad face filled his vid-screen.

Beck Brackenstone winced at the sadness in her voice. "Ma, you have to promise me that you won't go bothering my mate. We're courting."

Beck's wooing skills were seriously lacking, but having Ma poke her nose into it would make things even worse.

"But the Half-Moon folks need me."

Beck bit his lip. His mate led the Half-Moon Guild. The group of assassins had recently moved to Charybdis Station, and they really *could* use some friends.

Poor Ninetta was recuperating from losing part of her leg. She had a lot of healing to do before she could be fitted for a robotic prosthesis. She needed some love and attention.

"Okay, okay. You can go visit Half-Moon, but you can't talk about me to Beol."

She gasped in outrage. "You're my only son. What else would I talk about?"

"Your five daughters? The million kids you've adopted over the years? Pops?"

"Don't you take that tone with me, young man."

"Ma." Beck wasn't proud of the whine in his voice.

She made a face at him. "Fine. I'll do my best to avoid your mate, but I'm still feeding the rest of them. They need me."

Beck knew that was as good as he could hope for. Beck had met his mate a few weeks ago, and ever since then, Ma and Pops had been pestering him about bringing Beol to *officially* meet them. Then there were his sisters and Selene and Hack. Beck almost felt sorry for the poor guy.

"Well, now that we've settled that, are you going to explain your behavior?"

Beck frowned. "Huh?"

Ma narrowed her eyes. "Ever since you moved into your house, you've been hiding something. You don't even let your pa go into your workshop."

Beck yelped and grabbed his tail. "Hiding? There's nothing to hide. Nothing at all."

Ma's eyes softened. "Oh, Beckie Boo. You're a horrible liar."

"I am not." Beck sniffed.

She smiled indulgently. "Of course, you're not, baby boy."

Her eyes narrowed and she gave him a hard look. "Now, explain yourself. For months, I go by your house and your door is locked and your drapes pulled. Normally, that wouldn't stop me, but you even locked me out of your security system."

She huffed. "Your pa and I both couldn't hack into it."

Beck rolled his eyes. "I need my privacy. That's all."

"Hmm." Ma gave him a considering look. "A few days ago, I saw a woman and a man sneak in the back, Beck. I didn't recognize them, but they looked shifty. Are you in trouble, baby boy? I know you aren't cheating on your mate, so that can't be it."

Oh gods. Beck groaned. "Ma, just don't worry about it, alright? They're just some of my friends."

"Then why did they duck behind a bush when Leti and I walked by?"

"Uh, they're just really shy?"

"Beck."

"Oh no, look at the time. I need to go, Ma. I love you, and I'll see you at the wedding next week."

He turned the vid-screen off when Ma began protesting and buried his face in his hands. What was he going to do? Ma was starting to notice things, and she would tell everyone. Beck hated hiding things from his friends and family.

Dr. Bloop gave a soft woof and wiggled around Beck's feet. His puppy was only a couple of months old, but they had bonded hard. Beck adored him.

"Oh, Bloopy. Ma will figure things out soon. I just know it."

Buy Here: https://amzn.to/2HpI4vH

Excerpt from *Falling for the Omega*, Book One of the Hobson Hills Omegas

Carter loaded the last of his tools into his new work van and shut the door. His first day in his new profession was off to a good start. He had three clients to see today and eight spread out during the rest of the week.

Finally getting his plumbing license had been a good idea, even if his perfect, wealthy family hated the idea of him being a plumber.

Hell, they had also hated the idea of him being a soldier and of him moving out of state when he came back injured. They pretty much hated every decision he made.

The crisp fall wind was cold, but the gold, brown, and red leaves on the trees and ground made the cold worth dealing with. Autumn in Maine sure wasn't the same as autumn in Georgia, but so far, he was damn happy with the move. There was a peace here amongst the trees that he hadn't managed to find anywhere else.

"Hi, Mr. Neighbor!"

A child's voice came from behind him, startling Carter. He spun around, stumbling a bit on his prosthesis, and faced the little girl standing a few feet from his van.

She looked about five or six, with two black braids, caramel skin, and a freckled nose. When she smiled brightly, he saw a small gap between her two front teeth.

A black and gray miniature schnauzer sat at her feet, gaze stern and trained on him.

He looked around and didn't see any adults. His little half acre tract was quite a ways back from the road, nestled between a good-sized apple orchard on one side and a thick forest on the other.

Where the hell had this little girl come from?

"My name's Olive, and I brought you a welcome basket. I made it myself, but Daddy made you one too. He's gonna bring it tonight. I wanted you to get mine first, 'cause it's from me and then we'll be best friends." The little girl paused to take a breath. Her wide brown eyes sparkled and met his straight on, innocent and fearless. "We'll be best friends forever."

She didn't even seem to see the scars along the side of his face. The burn marks had already made two kids cry at the grocery store yesterday. Both times, the parents had been too embarrassed to apologize. They just grabbed their kids and ran.

"Uh, where's your daddy, Olive?" His voice was

deep and cracked, broken by the scarring on his neck. Her adoring stare was starting to freak him out a little. He'd never really been around kids.

"He's at home," she answered and handed him the basket. "See what I brought you? Look, look, look."

"Do you know your phone number? Maybe we could give your daddy a call," Carter said, taking the basket from Olive. He pulled the small hand towel from the top and almost dropped the basket. "Is that a hedgehog?"

"Yep! That's Hodges the hedgehog. He wanted to come visit too. Oh and this is Winston," she said and knelt to pet the small dog.

"Okay, your number?" He tried to keep his gruff voice kind. No sense in scaring the kid.

"Olive! Olive Persephone Wilson! Where are you?" A man's voice called from the orchard, full of panic and desperation.

"Uh oh," Olive said. She hurriedly looked around, then darted behind his van, Winston following her. "That's Daddy." She poked her head out and stared hard. "Tell. Him. Nothing."

She quickly hid again when a young omega rushed out of the orchard. He was her father, had to be. He looked just like her.

Carter suddenly couldn't catch his breath. The man in front of him was simply adorable. He was short and well formed, a little chubby. His black hair fell in curls around his face, and his wide hazel eyes contrasted beautifully with his caramel skin. The same freckles that decorated his daughter's nose, fell across his own.

Where it looked cute on the kid, on her father... Bad thoughts, Carter! Bad thoughts!

"Have you seen a little girl? Black hair? Brown eyes? Miniature schnauzer with her? Maybe a hedgehog?"

Carter stared at the handsome man, mouth gaping, for too long.

The man frowned at him, tilting his head. "Are you alright?" His shy smile revealed the small gap between his front teeth.

Oh fuck, he was so damn perfect. He met Carter's eyes too, didn't even glance at the scars.

"Mister?"

Carter shook his head and did his best to pull himself together. He smiled, as best he could with the scar tissue, and nodded toward the van, holding a finger to his lips, encouraging the man to keep quiet.

Olive's father rolled his eyes and stomped around the van. A squealing Olive ran from her hiding spot and hid behind Carter, hugging him around the waist.

"Mr. Neighbor, save me!" Her giggling told him she wasn't too worried about her father catching her.

"Olive, you scared me to death running off like that." Her father really did look worried. "What have I told you about leaving the house without me?"

"But daddy," she whined. "I wanted to meet Mr. Neighbor. We're best friends now, and I gave him a welcome basket. I was being hospital."

Carter frowned. Hospital?

"Hospitable, baby girl, and it doesn't matter. You are too little to be wandering around by yourself and talking to strangers. No television time this week, and you have to clean out Pooka and Banjo's stalls on Saturday."

Olive gave a big sigh and leaned her forehead into Carter's leg. "Okay, Daddy, but it was worth it. I have a new best friend now."

The man met Carter's stare, a question in his eyes. Carter nodded and gave his best half smile.

"Well, maybe our new neighbor would like to come over for dinner one night? So that we can meet him properly," the man said.

"Yay! Mr. Neighbor, can you come tonight? Daddy's gonna make apple dumplins for dessert."

Carter smiled at the little girl and nodded. "Yeah, if it's okay with your dad."

The man smiled and nodded eagerly. "That would be great. I hardly ever get to cook for anyone but Olive." He gave a flustered look and held out his hand. "Oh, I forgot. My name is Elijah Wilson. I live in the farmhouse with the orchard. Of course, you've met Olive."

Carter shook his hand, touch lingering longer than it should. He was reluctant to release him but finally did. "Yeah, I'm Carter Benson. Just moved here from Georgia."

"Wow, so Maine's probably a bit different, huh?"

"Yeah, but all the colors on the trees? And ya'll actually have snow. I've never seen much of it."

"You say that like snow is a good thing." Elijah shuddered. "Well, welcome to Hobson Hill. I see Olive already gave you a welcome basket."

Carter looked back in it. "There's a hedgehog in

there." His coarse voice was getting rougher as he spoke. He wasn't used to talking so much. Doctors said it was good for him to do though.

"I put cider in there for you. It's in my favorite big girl cup, the one with Moana. There's also butter from Pooka and some of Daddy's bread. It's so yummy!"

"Thanks, Olive. I appreciate it," Carter said. The little girl still hung on his leg, smiling up at him. She was a cute one, he acknowledged, even though she was clearly a little crazy. It was a good crazy though.

"Your alpha won't mind me coming," Carter asked Elijah.

The man winced and lowered his eyes. "I don't have an Alpha, so no, that won't be a problem."

Carter was surprised. Happy, but surprised. This adorable man had to be beating them off with a stick. Of course, some folks thought poorly about single omegas, and some alphas refused to even speak to them. Idiots.

"I guess I'll see you tonight. What time?"

"Oh, is six okay?" Elijah's confidence seemed to bounce back at Carter's question.

"That's fine. I better get to work."

"Yes, of course," Elijah said and pulled Olive off Carter's leg. "Come on, Olive. We better get back to the house. We need to get you to school."

"Okay. Bye, Carter, love you!" The little girl and her dog ran off through the orchard.

"I swear it's exhausting keeping up with her," Elijah sighed. Carter smiled and held the hedgehog out to him. "Thanks," he said, taking Hodges and smiling shyly. "See you tonight. Have a good day at work."

Carter stood frozen as he watched Elijah walk away. He was in trouble. Big, wonderful trouble.

Buy Here: https://amzn.to/2BgWURV

Excerpt from *The Guppy Prince*, book one in The Silver Isles.

Dover Rees floated in the deepest part of his creek, enjoying the rushing sound of the waterfall to his right. Sunlight filtered through the water, glinting off the deep blue of his guppy tail. His thin and delicate caudal fin spread out like an elegant fan, dancing through the warm water as he swayed.

His favorite smooth and colorful pebbles were strewn around below him, and he admired the shells he had collected and placed beside them. Dover breathed deeply and enjoyed the peace and quiet. No one mocked him or bossed him around. No one watched him with cold eyes and hidden smirks. *I wish I could stay here forever.*

Sudden movement beside him jarred him from his thoughts and he laughed when Chubber grabbed a bright pink stone in his small brown paws and swam away. Dover's otter friend liked to steal Dover's shinies then share them with him again later.

A brook trout swam past him and Dover debated grabbing it for an early lunch, but he wasn't too hungry yet. Lately, he'd been eating less and less, and he couldn't make himself care.

The quiet water around him hummed as Nami quickly swam to him. His best friend's guppy tail was a lovely pink pattern with black dots, and her short black hair floated around her head. The cat with a mermaid tail on her black tankini top made him smile. He loved her purr-maid shirts.

"Have you eaten today, Your Highness?" she asked.

Dover scowled. "Don't call me that."

"When you're acting like a pouting asswipe, that's what you get called." Nami wrapped her arms around him and settled her head on his shoulder. "What's wrong with you, Dover?"

Dover had no answer for her. All he knew was he felt empty inside and it was harder and harder to get up in the morning. "I think I ate some bad clams."

"Every day for the past two months?" Nami leaned back and glared at him, her dark eyes seeing right through him.

Chubber came to his rescue, swimming in between them and wrapping his lean body across Dover's shoulders. "Chubber wants to get a snack."

Nami sighed, bubbles filling the water around her. "Mom is in your cottage making lunch. You're worrying us, bluetail."

Dover stroked a hand through her hair, then shoved

her down and pushed up, swimming toward the surface.

"Damn it!" Nami swam after him.

He laughed, heart warming. *Someone cares about me.* It wasn't his family, but Nami and her mom were closer to him than his parents or any of his twelve siblings.

Chubber clung to his back and nibbled on his ear until he mentally apologized. Chubber cared about him the most.

His creek was deep, but it didn't take him long to reach the surface. Shauna waited for them on the shore, hands on her hips. Chubber's mother, Shell, stood on her hind legs beside the mermaid, chirping loudly. Uh oh. He really was in trouble.

"You didn't eat breakfast, did you?" The wind blew strands of Shauna's pink hair across her face, ruining her glare.

"Sorry, Shauna."

She sighed. "I made your favorite."

"Grilled shrimp salad?" Dover's stomach rumbled.

"With avocado, papaya, mango, and pineapple. All your favorites." Shauna gave him a soft look. "Come eat, bluetail."

Dover summoned his human legs and a few seconds later, walked out of the creek, naked, with Chubber clinging to his shoulder. Shauna handed him a deep teal sarong, and he tied it about his waist.

Shell crawled up his leg and into his arms, then rubbed her slick furry face against his. She was a bit heavier than Chubber, but he was still a baby.

"Why does he get all the loving?" Nami asked, grumbling as she tied a sarong around her own waist.

Dover chuckled when Shauna arched an eyebrow at her daughter. "Did you say something, sweetness?"

"No, ma'am," Nami said, wincing.

"You two come eat lunch." Shauna turned around and walked toward Dover's large cottage.

Dover closed his eyes for a moment and savored the feel of the moss-covered rocks under his feet, and the comfortable breeze quickly drying his curly blue hair. He loved his home so much. It was his sanctuary.

Buy Here: https://amzn.to/2q9Q8en